EXACTING CLAM No. 4 — Spring 2022

I0667977

CONTENTS

Front cover: "Spring" by Kathleen Nicholls

Exacting Clam is a quarterly publication from Sagging Meniscus.

Senior Editors: Aaron Anstett, Jesi Bender, Jeff Chon, Elizabeth Cooperman, Tyler C. Gore, Charles Holdefer, Kurt Luchs, M.J. Nicholls, Doug Nufer, Thomas Walton

Executive Editor: Guillermo Stitch

Publisher: Jacob Smullyan

exactingclam.com

LETTERS & COMPLAINTS

Dear Editors,

I have been unable to subscribe to your lateral literary fascicle for the last two issues for very heavy agricultural reasons, if you observe.

Pak choi winded me in the autumn. Taproot mould—a charred mushy taint six centimetres down, inviting to malign invertebrate nibblers—savaged seven hectares of my turnips, eclipsing the Portsmouth Rot of 1978 that commenced the craze for cheaply tossed Chinese cabbage, flooding the market with a sickly fungible exotic spiciness irresistible to the English palate. The steady harrumphing in agribusiness following Brexit's public capture had kneaded a sense of warm complacency into the largely cretinous minds of turnip traders, causing us to lean on our laurels and hardy ways to weather any hypothetical storms ... thus utterly unprepared for this heinous taproot assault.

I had always sneered at rivals recruiting taproot monitors (burly Mongolians on hand to ensure a virile cultivar length, to hunt and kill any hairy-backed nibblers nesting in the radicles, to keep the layers of grot to a washable minimum) to sentry their cabbage progress. Those farmers who employed these strapping farmhands to farmhandle their mouldering roots swerved the pak choi pounding (from Vietnam, this time) and continue to pay their dues to the Conversative Party as the rest of us pack our kitbags for the city.

(Yes, sirs, my farm folded with the retractable back-snap of a multiplex chair).

This is why I would advise your rustic readers to consider the wisdom of investing in an experienced vegetable watcher from a landlocked socialist republic. You cannot predict the evils that lurk there under the loam, and you cannot trust Mother Nature not to poison your lot with sudden upturns in soil moisture.

You may therefore appreciate, editor, my short-term unperusal of your literary orbit, and excuse the pungency of my neglect.

Yours,

Draywort MacAdam

Dear "Editors",

We are all aware of the difficulties that pronounced size differential can present to an intimate relationship, and I for one need no convincing that this grossly underreported and neglected matter is needful of serious address in literature. Imagine my disappointment, then, upon reading, in your Winter 2021 issue, Colin Gee's "Dear John", which takes exactly the wrong approach to the subject.

Gee's piece, a Dear John letter written by a woman to a partner (conveniently named John) who has gradually shrunk to the point of being microscopic, indulges conspicuously in the most egregious sort of ableist mockery of short people: exploiting our (supposed) sexual insufficiencies, our squeaky high-pitched voices, the challenges we may face in traversing distances, etc., for cheap laughs.

(I write here in the first-person plural not because I am myself a person of slight stature, corporeally, but because I identify with communities that welcome and include little people, and as they are part of us, so too do they participate in me, in a small way. God bless us, every one.)

We may not all be literally shrinking—though, whether due to age or transhumanist experimentation gone awry, some surely are—but a great many of us are expanding. The probability that we may experience this inflation at vastly different rates means that a significant number are indeed shrinking relative to their partner, leading to painful problems of a kind it is evidently not beneath Gee to stoop to milk for crass entertainment value.

This alone renders the piece, and your publication of it, reprehensible. But Gee doesn't leave it there. No—along the way he also manages to sling dirt at women of substance: "Maybe that is the real crux of the problem. You made me feel fat, John. I am a little woman with a flat tummy, and you made me feel fat and gross!"

One might easily conclude that fat-shaming is what this heartless flash is really about: making light of those so tiny as to be invisible is a transparent facade for a misogynist attack on the buxom, the expansive, and the fleshily incorrigible.

Yours,

J Sprat

Pamela Ryder

Abilene

We took up taking horses, mustangs first since they was free for the taking, running loose and fierce from what some say since forever and breeding out in every kind and color, like the little herd of broncs we caught up with crossing Carrizo Creek. None we caught was a Choctaw pony like the one I'd been riding, but there was pintos and paints, bays, sorrel grays, an appaloosa roan or two, and one buckskin dun, and then a few of them with coats I couldn't name or there wasn't names invented. And we roped saddle horses right out of the remudas when the wranglers weren't looking and sometimes even when they were, and hell, didn't we even steal ponies where they stood tied to the rail outside saloons where the cowhands what owned them were inside drinking and whoring and carrying on. We ran horses off ranches and we ran them off the cavalry forts, some being riding ponies and some just recent tame and some being wild-tailed mustangs right off the plains. Most we drove them clear across the Territory to Tucumcari into Texas and we crossed the Prairie Dog Town Fork where flocks of little bluebills rose up like dark clouds when we splashed on through and then straight south and across the Rio Grande into Mexico and the big cattle spreads that took as many horses we could fetch them. When the law got too close in Texas, we did our rustling in Arizona along the dry Santa Cruz, got them ponies shoed up by the smith at Fort Grant, and took them into Mexico by way of Nogales. Some we sold off across the Texas border in Kansas where they would go on by rail from Abilene. But one time I went all the way to Abilene. One time. We drove those ponies out of the traps and up the ramps. Some of them was mares with their little foals trying to hold close to their mamas, but all of them, all of them, getting whupped into the boxcars and packed in every which way so they couldn't stand but with their heads hung on the backs of each other and when the big doors slid shut they were on their way to cities in the East to be spending the rest of their lives not even being rode but dragging coal carts and wagons over the stone streets where they would never more see a blade of buffalo grass or drink from rivers or feel wind not full of smoke and soot. No more life like that, no. Now it would be blinders on their eyes and getting whipped and beat until they dropped. I seen it myself. And that one time when I drove them all the way through Kansas, I seen them loaded up at Abilene. That one time. Some wouldn't go, and that would be just the start of more whipping to come. When those boxcar doors slid closed, one of them he gets his big horse eye up against an opening in the slats. I knew that eye. I knew that color. It was the buckskin dun. I remember when I roped him up around Carrizo Creek. Gave me a hell of a chase that one, the buckskin dun. And now there he is looking at me through the slats and at the Choctaw pony where I'm sitting. The train starts to go and that's when I hear them wild things in the boxcar start to stomping as if they was running, as if they got themselves loose and free and gone. The train going on then. Pulling away. And me, I'm not knowing if what I'm hearing is the big smoking locomotive leaving out the station yard or is it them ponies that's screaming inside that boxcar dark. I heard it in my head a good while way after it was gone, I did. That one time I drove those ponies clear through to Abilene.

DAVID HENNINGHAM

Kittewake

From *Foulness* (Unbound 2022)

kittee-wa-aaake, kitte-wa-aaake,
tucks in his neck and
  brooding
dips black tips into the buffeting.
Looks inland,
    out to the island,
rejects them both for auxiliary silt—
  arcs
    alights on the silt,
      scoops great armfuls of air on the mile down
        shoos the air cushion away with his wings
      grasps at solid sea-bed silt with his feet,
leaves his grace in the cloakroom
  takes the ticket
waddles travel-stiff on the tide-ribboned silt,
  inspects a black wormcast—
a tourist in the museum of fine art.

'There never was a future for alchemy, not while we could transmute base instincts into gold.' That's what de la Cour said to me. 'Alchemists were too ambitious. But take the men in ballistics. They take the same lead the alchemists did and, merely by firing it into some poor sod on the battlefield, they fill their banks to bursting with solid gold.'

That took longer than anticipated. De la Cour kept going off on tangents. He wandered about his office, pausing at his desk to crack hazelnuts with a tarnished steel nutcracker—a simple sloppy hinge—but he never returned to his point. It was as if his thoughts came out of the nuts.

And now, announcing himself with a sharp *rap* on the car window, Commandant de la Cour's grinning face has appeared on the other side of it. *What on earth can he have to say to me here he couldn't already have said in his office?*

'Wait a moment please, driver.' I struggle to wind the window down with my left hand.

'You will need this, corporal,' de la Cour says, slipping an envelope through the sliver of open window. 'This is The Matter In Hand.'

Even as he is saying this, de la Cour pats the hollow rump of the car and it duly pulls away from the kerb, towards the gatehouse that marks the exit from the red-brick barracks.

It wasn't only the nuts. De la Cour plucked a lead musket ball from his desk and held it up to the light for me to examine but, as I reached him, he snatched it down to his chest, squeezing the musket ball tight in his fist.

'It takes a supernova to make gold ordinarily,' he said. 'Did you know that? The languid death of a modest star like our sun just won't do the trick. But with a little puff of gunpowder energy, the men in ballistics achieve the same, here, on terra firma.'

A little toss, then de la Cour carefully placed the flat face of the musket ball, the face that remembers its discharge, back on his desk. As the briefing wore on, it sat at rest among half a dozen pieces of corroded shot, as celestial bodies might while Euclid slept.

The driver's feet work a moment's pause from the pedals as deftly as a tango dancer while the sentry raises the barrier, ushering us into residential streets flanked by bungalows. I sit back in the bucket seat, releasing its musty odour, looking at de la Cour's tardy envelope and wondering if its late delivery was a dirty trick.

As the car makes a right turn, I lift the ungummed flap and squeeze its edges until the envelope opens like an eye. I slide two fingers in and retrieve—*an aerial photograph.* A circular birds' eye view capturing some kind of peninsula on its left, and several enormous sandbanks out to sea

4

on the right. Foulness Island, naturally. It looks remarkably like a finch's wing stretched out for examination, that is, if the island forms the scapulars and Maplin Sands provides the primary and secondary flights. These are de la Cour's firing ranges—the sandbanks he just told me about, at length, upon which experimental weapons have been proved for a century.

'I know what they will have told you,' de la Cour said to me, dismissively. 'But our business here at Shoeburyness is *debunking* ballistics. Finding out just how far and fast something will *really* go, and what it will accomplish when it gets there. Take this, for example.'

With one hand he took, from between the nuts and musket balls, a small damp piece of cast steel. It was so dense I was obliged to receive it with both hands. There was a dent in the middle the size of a golf ball. He rocked on the balls of his feet. 'One would have expected a bit more damage than that,' he said, 'if one were to believe the manufacturer's claims. Right now I've got half a dozen men mudlarking off Foulness Island, retrieving bits of their prototype. Another assault on the public purse has been repelled.'

I look out of the car window, wondering when we will pass through the fag-burn perimeter of the aerial photograph onto Foulness Island. Outside there are only civilian bungalows, hunkered down as if afraid of stray ordnance, and between these clusters, brown fields. We continue along rough ochre roads, their black seams protruding like canine gums.

'This!—however—is what we're aiming for,' de la Cour had said, crossing the room to remove another piece of steel plate from the wall where it hung proudly among watercolours and photographs of men posing with ordnance, as if for magazine advertisements. 'Guess the range on that one, corporal,' he said, returning to me and swapping it for the dented one.

He leaned back against the front of his desk. There was a "crack" and he picked through the ruins of the shell on his palm for the kernel. I held the steel up to the light, half an inch thick with an esplanade of seven holes in it. Of course I have no idea about such things so, for no particular reason, I thought of the distance between my flat in London and the parade of shops.

'Thirty yards?'

'Thirty yards!' he laughed. 'Closer to a hundred. You might have seen those in action during the War.'

The car enters a village held together by a T-junction. My eyes snatch its name from the blurred sign: GREAT WAKERING. A quick heel-drop from the driver and we lurch right, away from the squat stone church, in accordance with a signpost indicating FOULNESS.

That wasn't the only piece of trophy steel displayed on the Commandant's wall, among silver gelatine prints. De la Cour uncrossed his ankles and levered himself up from the edge of the desk, leading me by the elbow to admire them.

'Our patron saint,' he said to me, tapping a picture of a portly man in a top hat standing next to a small tripod. Another much larger version of that tripod enclosed them, as one might see in a stained glass window—a tiny version of the church one is standing in resting on its patron saint's arm.

'William Hale, here, was a self-taught inventor. Colchester born and bred. He came down here to Shoeburyness to test these revolutionary stickless war-rockets. Lieutenant-Colonel Shrapnel followed in his footsteps and the upshot is no window pane in the parish predates eighteen-sixty-one.'

De la Cour proudly indicated another of the Old Gunnery School's old boys, a gastropodic gun christened "Big Will". It looked like something between a church bell and a diving bell, riveted to the extreme front of a pair of rocking horse runners. A bored gunner stood in front for scale.

De la Cour moved on to a neighbouring photograph. 'This eighty-tonner always reminds me of a Madonna and Child.' One vast gun was mounted on a railway sleigh with a tiny cannon parked in front, yet the sentiment transformed the loitering, bearded gunner into Joseph—made of different stuff to his wife and son. A ram-rod formed from the best part of a tree was laid in front.

I glanced back at Big Will and imagined the monster rocking back and forth after firing, an untuned ringing, nodding without sense like a shell-shocked imbecile. I was becoming fascinated.

'And this one, sir?' I asked, pointing to a gun that hung like a puppet from a cradle of pulleys and cables as it was lifted from a boat.

'A hundred-tonner! You have a good eye, corporal,' he chuckled. 'See that barge? The *Gog*, "gathering them together to battle, the number of whom is as the sand of the sea." But, alas,' said de la Cour, turning away from his peculiar gallery, 'that was all in the Golden Age.' He returned to his position against his desk and sighed. 'As Archimedes said, perhaps to his wife: "give me a lever big enough and I'll move the earth for you." You know, my worker bees up on Foulness Island, on the back of an envelope in the canteen, they will actually calculate the exact length required to lever the earth? That's their idea of leisure! You see what I'm up against?'

The brakes wince as we halt at the first military structure since Shoeburyness barracks—a small building signposted LANDWICK LODGE. Beyond a chain-link fence two stocky horses, one chestnut the other white, eat crab apples that dangle from a tree. A sentry leans in the passenger window while the driver deals with the formalities. The car glides forwards again as we are waved through the wire. We are enclosed in the sterile area.

'You see what I'm up against,' de la Cour said, as he reached behind and picked up his nutcracker. 'What I wouldn't give for some simple iron and shot. But, these days, needs must we act faster! The government is compelled to be more deliberate. The gamekeeper has turned poacher, as it were. We can't just pop a physics-package ...'

Wait, we didn't cross water—'Driver? Is *this* the island?'

'Not yet, sir. The rolling bridge'll take us over Havengore Creek.'

'... We can't just pop a physics-package in the first-class post!' de la Cour said. 'Aeronautics! New-fangled communicadoes. Vulgar modern HQs, all concrete, steel and glass right down to the lavatory brushes—they seem confident enough about their future, but one wonders what kind of future it will be for the rest of us. You follow?'

'I'm not sure that I do, sir,' I said.

'They seem determined to put the Industrial Revolution in their shade, but if you ask me, they're more likely to deposit us all back in the Dark Ages. So many lessons not learned from the first time around. Combustion is essentially a myth, yet people persist in believing that when a thing burns it disappears!' He reached behind for a nut and waved it in the air to suggest something evaporating. 'But when a thing is burned it becomes compounded with elements in the air, yes? A lump of coal, once burned, is heavier than before, did you know that?'

'Sir—'

'—How much more, then, with *fission*, has combustion become a complete misapprehension? When uranium is simply shuffled along the periodic table a bit? Uranium, neptunium, plutonium. Transmutation. All that energy! Finally alchemy *really genuinely works* and we should all be living like kings, really. Instead we make a *pluto-nium bomb*! It's like cracking somebody's skull with the Venus de—BOLLOCKS!'

De la Cour groaned as the remains of a musket ball crumbled from the nutcracker in his hand.

I leaned forward and peered over the driver's shoulder at a Tarmac tombstone. A mast slid nimbly behind the rolling bridge that stood at ninety degrees to the earth, the boat itself too small to be visible. The bridge remained at odds with the world for a long time after its passage, until the summit imperceptibly began to shrink. The silhouette became trapezoid; the bridge had begun its descent. It took less than a minute for the bridge and its clockwork teeth to be absorbed by the horizontal plane.

It was as if we had crossed a drawbridge into a castle, an impression that the grass embankment, a system of sea defences, only confirmed. Between them and our road lay grassy mounds of the type used for storing field ordnance.

We drove at a mandated walking pace with nothing else but flat fields on either side for about half a mile. At last a landmark appeared to our left, something that also glowed on the southwest edge of my aerial photograph, distorted by the limit of the lens. Cross-hatched by the chain-link fence. A long thin white hangar, semi-circular in profile, becoming fatter at one end like the plunger of a hypodermic syringe. I'd not seen a structure like this before. This was built for a sin-gular purpose. Faded blue gates appeared that I presumed would take the car to the structure, but we drove straight past. Yet we had finally entered the photograph.

I glanced right, towards the sea. A deserted wooden building stood out, a black tooth against the island's grassy gumline. I looked down at the photograph and determined the military base should be just ahead.

Suddenly, with that same blow to the senses of having nearly fallen asleep, our road was once more flanked by civilian dwellings—windows open, washing flapping on lines, a child's tricycle abandoned in the centre of a lawn. Where I thought the photograph had shown a military base, there was a bus stop. We paused at the crossroads, an idyllic country hamlet embedded in the heart of a military installation. *It must be a training ground*, I thought, *like the one on Salisbury Plain*.

Yet, when the car took a right turn towards the sea, passing more cottages with tidy front gar-dens abundant with September blooms, a man could be seen washing his car. On his driveway. As if he lived in Shoeburyness, or Southend, and not on an island encircled by barbed wire.

'What is this place, driver?'

'Churchend, sir.'

'A village?'

He scrutinised me in the mirror. 'Yes, sir.'

'A *normal* village?'

The driver did not contradict me. Nor, per-haps, would he have contradicted anyone who recommended me for the post of village idiot.

The cottages soon made way for farm build-ings and, as if we had been traversing a Möbius strip, a set of Victorian red brick barracks ap-peared, clad in the same limestone braiding as de la Cour's garrison, but a lower rank. These bar-racks parallaxed across the fields towards us. We were the same distance from the village as the vil-lage had been from the bridge.

I climbed from the vehicle, my eyes still fixed on the photograph. Examining from above the old church and the village shop we had just passed.

The sound of gravel grinding beneath the departing car's tyres gave way to oscillating footfalls behind me. I turned and saw her approaching—an attractive young woman in service dress.

'Miss Bradshaw,' she said, touching her cap softly. 'Major Edulis is sorry but he couldn't meet you in person, sir. He is engaged at present. I have been instructed to show you round.'

She turned about, her long, thick plait settling between her shoulder blades. I quickly returned my photograph to its envelope and slipped it into my satchel, then made to follow, but almost cannoned into her as she paused and looked back to say: 'You're very late, you know.'

'I'm sorry,' I said. 'Commandant de la Cour's briefing took much longer than expected.'

I drew up beside her as we crossed the gravel apron towards a grass embankment that divided the base from the sea, a hop knotted in her hips that brought to mind greyhounds.

'I hope you weren't waiting long,' I said. 'The Commandant didn't half go on.'

'Major Edulis asked me to show you the radar station, sir,' said Miss Bradshaw, 'but there isn't much time.'

We were approaching what might once have been a grand villa but now looked like a giant had sliced off its first storey with a cheese wire; only a long red-brick gallery remained. Closer inspection revealed some lintels were missing entirely and most of the sandstone flourishes chiselled through carelessly, leaving eyeless cherubs and torn scrolls. A corrugated iron roof sat across the top of the walls, pitched at a shallow angle upon rough wooden sandwich beams that assumed the role of the second floor.

I peered inside through the glass. The stained plaster ceiling bulged downwards as if it was full of tea. Lath ribs poked through wherever rain had found its course. On the other side of the villa, facing the grassy embankment, a central semicircle of weather-blasted stone marked out where there must once have been a veranda. Two lumpen lions stared at the sea defences, their features carried off by the rain. Peering in through the broken panes I could see stone steps built into the brick wall, curving around a corner, butted up against the corrugated sheets above, going nowhere.

'This is supposed to be a radar station?' I said, but Miss Bradshaw was gone. She had already turned away and was heading back the way we had come. I peered quickly through the smeared window again, but if there were any of the electrical plant essential for a radar station, it was better hidden than the Coalhouse Fort job. I followed her.

I caught up with her beside a dozen black wooden sheds laid out in two rows. 'I look forward to seeing you make it disappear, sir,' she said.

This is a common mistake, so I replied: 'That isn't how camouflage typically works. It's not about making things disappear.'

We left the sheds behind. Their tarred walls warped by successive barrages of sun and precipitation. Typical temporary structures, remaining long after their builders have departed. The cabins smelled of cut grass, oil, rust, dust, old summers.

I continued. 'Yes, during the War we'd lay reflective surfaces in a field to suggest a bend in the river, to throw off the Luftwaffe's navigators—wheezes like that.' We continued across the apron we had set off from, towards much more recent buildings. 'But spy planes are much more advanced these days,' I explained. 'Heinkels were little more than one of those sheds back there with wings attached. One now has to accept that the ground can be read more fluently from the air. The question becomes, what do you want the ground to say?'

'Whatever can you mean, sir?' she said, placing a hand on my back to steer me away from the double doors at the front of a modern brick building, towards its side entrance.

'The war's gone cold,' I said. 'We're communicating with the skies. Everything inside an installation's sterile area should be designed to *display* our capabilities, not hide them.'

Miss Bradshaw held open the side door for me, leading into the block. Straight ahead was another door leading through to an atrium. Its outside edge was paved, perhaps the path had once been open to the elements, but now it has been enclosed with a wooden conservatory to form a corridor. Wooden frames looked onto a central courtyard with a concrete bird table and a bare bush twisted to a fist by coastal gusts.

'But I don't understand,' she said quietly, as her heels became a clock's second hand clicking around the corridor. 'If everything is in plain sight, how does that count as camouflage?'

'Ah, now that's where it gets interesting,' I said. 'Take the aerodrome at Welford. The Yanks have struck it out with a jet-age airstrip. That's like striking through a *sentence on a page*, you see. But what does it mean now?'

Looking into the rooms connected by this corridor, there didn't seem to be much going on. Two cooks were smoking and drinking tea. In the next there were two Privates, one looking out the window while the other, sat at a desk, licked his pencil and put it to paper. Miss Bradshaw slowed to a halt outside a frosted-glass office door, and I wheeled past to stand beside her.

'Obscuring something can make it more legible,' I said. 'Good camouflage is like writing for someone with a reading disease—writing for word blindness.'

'Sorry, I don't follow,' she said, distracted. Raised voices from inside the office were competing for her attention. Then she turned to face me, frowning slightly, as if she hadn't quite heard before. 'What on earth is *word blindness*?' she asked.

Assuming we were waiting for the voices in the room to cease, I went on. 'It's just that: a disease that inhibits a child who is learning to read.'

'There are diseases that stop children *reading* now?'

'Yes.'

'But there's always been slower kids,' she said, looking back at the door.

One particular voice beyond the door was repeating the same muffled rhythm.

'Well,' I said. 'We know now that it *can* be a medical condition.'

'Really, sir?' Miss Bradshaw flicked her plait into the middle of her back with her hand and looked at me with a new level of attention. 'But why haven't I heard of this before?'

'It's specialist knowledge, I suppose—not clinical,' I said. 'When I first made the comparison between word blindness and camouflage, at the Ministry, it was considered something of a breakthrough.' I chuckled, thinking back for a moment. 'I first heard about it from a Research Fellow at university.'

'This fellah, did he cure it?'

'I—I don't know. But the *point* is, his subjects often described words on a page as "dancing". He would strike out words with lines and shapes and found that, to these subjects, the words could become more legible, not less.' In the office a second man's voice breached and sounded in the relentless waves of the first. 'But my point is,' I said, 'that's really how camouflage works these days. *Striking out* what one hopes *will* be understood. Measures, counter-measures, counter-countermeasures—but look here.' I glanced at the office door. 'Do you think we should come back another time?'

'Hmm?'

'They sound—preoccupied.'

Miss Bradshaw's shoulder flinched, apparently about to raise a hand and knock on the door, then hesitating. We waited until it became quiet. We both leaned forward slightly, straining to listen for any further noises from within.

I studied the name plate, MAJOR EDULIS, and recalled the last thing de la Cour had told me: 'Edulis is a bit of a funny fish,' de la Cour had said. 'I was schooled in the *other* place, but that can't fully explain the antipathy.' Then he turned his back on me before adding regretfully, 'I wouldn't be surprised if this were our Major's last posting.'

Miss Bradshaw held the office door open and I entered ahead of her. I made straight for Major Edulis, clearly identified by his olive-green service dress. He stood behind a wide wooden desk on the other side of the small room. He was leaning forward with both palms flat on the desk's varnished surface, staring at me confusedly.

Major Edulis shifted his weight to his feet and lifted a trembling right hand to smooth his thick, black moustache, with a firm symmetrical movement of his thumb and forefinger. Sweat clung to his forehead like sap. Wondering why he was standing like this, I stood at ease and glanced to his left-hand side where a girl sat perched on a stool with a jotter and pencil in her hands. She was in the same plain service uniform as Miss Bradshaw, yet my eyes registered a red gingham Alice band. She couldn't yet be twenty. She too stared at me. The wall behind them was featureless apart from a row of thick glass bricks high above their heads. To my left was a glass partition and doorway, presumably leading to a neighbouring orderly office.

Major Edulis remained silent. Increasingly unnerved, I glanced to my right, to see if I could guess what Miss Bradshaw made of the situation, but she wasn't there. I kept turning my upper body, my hands clasped behind my back, until I saw Miss Bradshaw out of the corner of my eye in the doorway, but before coming to her I had discovered a white-haired civilian man in his fifties, lounging in an easy chair beside the door we'd come in by. Presumably he was the man Major Edulis had been arguing with. I'd swept right past him on our way in.

There was a cough. I turned my upper body fully around in the other direction, only to see another young man wearing overalls, sitting in an easy chair on the other side of our entrance. There certainly were more people in here than I'd expected. Returning my face to the front, and looking at that space just above the officer's head they tend to find so agreeable, I came to the conclusion Major Edulis' briefing had not finished—it had merely become quieter. Yet, heedless, I had taken centre stage.

Major Edulis, emerging from his wrongfootedness, smoothed his moustache again.

'Ah, corporal,' he said, glancing at my cypress-green beret. 'Yes, we have been expecting you, haven't we.'

'Sir,' I said.

'Good. Good,' he said. Then, with forced levity: 'I can see you are keen to press on. I will leave you in Miss Bradshaw's capable hands.' He glanced at the white-haired man in the easy chair—'There are still some points to be agreed with Doctor Jääger.' The civilian man scoffed, then replied, in heavily accented English: 'Points to be rehearsed.'

Major Edulis kept his eyes fixed on him. 'Miss Bird,' he said. 'Would you be so good as to read back the Doctor's last words.'

The girl on the stool flicked hurriedly through her jotter, but before she could speak the Doctor interrupted again: 'And my last word on the subject is what it will be.'

Still standing at ease, I looked behind to the capable Miss Bradshaw for some direction. She had opened the door for our exit. Meanwhile, Miss Bird had located the Doctor's "words" and she began reading them nervously. I found myself instinctively in two minds, whether to make an exit as Major Edulis had instructed, or to dig my heels in, as it were, and await some clearer instructions. If I did not, when else could I expect to be briefed on the reasons for my coming to Foulness Island? Who else was going to explain the significance of this aerial photograph?

At first, as I waited, the white-haired Doctor continued disputing with poor Miss Bird, until his voice gradually stopped, realising with the others that I hadn't moved as expected. All eyes turned to me.

'Sir, if you don't mind,' I said, 'I was hoping to hear a little more about my brief before I go.'

'Miss Bradshaw will show you to your quarters, corporal,' he said firmly, 'I think I made that clear.'

'You did, sir, but I feel I must bring to your attention that a degree of confusion has entered the chain of command, sir.'

'My watch suggests,' he snapped, snatching a look at his wrist, 'that Commandant de la Cour detained you for the best part of the afternoon. What else need be said?'

I heard sniggering behind me, and caught sight of a suppressed smile on Miss Bird's face in front. I risked a quick look behind, but only gleaned that the young man I suspected of laughing was lighting a cigarette, and that Miss Bradshaw had become angry with me. Major Edulis was glaring at me too when I faced front again.

'But there isn't any radar—'

'—Radar, corporal? What do you want with radar!'

'I don't want radar, sir. It's just there can't be any radar equipment in those old buildings, sir.'

Major Edulis looked past my shoulder at Miss Bradshaw. She spoke immediately: 'I showed him, sir, I—'

'—Didn't *your* Ministry brief you on this, corporal?'

'Effectively not, sir. Colonel Gregory—'

'—What is that deplorable odour?' interrupted Major Edulis, looking over my shoulder again. Everyone in the room exchanged looks. Eventually the young man in overalls took the cigarette from his mouth and looked at it as if for the first time.

'Krzysztof?' said the Major. The young man didn't reply. 'The damn thing smells like rancid walnuts!'

The young man, Krzysztof, replied defensively in his faltering English: 'Imported, sir.'

'I scarcely think it was worth the bother,' replied the Major.

Krzysztof stood and walked slowly, perhaps impudently toward the desk. He extinguished the cigarette carefully in the Major's ashtray before returning it to his breast pocket for later.

Major Edulis trained his ire back on me while the young man returned to his seat: 'This is too bad. Really, too bad. Miss Bradshaw, please remove our new arrival to the orderly room until I can conclude this business with Doctor Jääger.'

I was startled by Miss Bradshaw's touch to my elbow. She steered me, not to the door we had come in by this time, but to the connecting door on my left hand. But just as she touched the handle the white-haired man, Doctor Jääger, stood up and spoke: 'Wait. Are you the man de la Cour sent for?'

I looked at him blankly. He flicked his eyes to the ceiling and emitted a long, high whistle.

Confused, I said: 'I don't know exactly who sent for me, sir.'

Doctor Jääger clicked his tongue with his teeth and took his seat again, watching us go with apparent interest.

Miss Bradshaw closed the door that connected Edulis' office to the Orderly Room with the small of her back, the textured glass rattling.

'What did you have to say that for!' she said, striding over to another door that would lead back to the atrium's glazed corridor. She opened it and peered into the corridor before closing it again. I was now standing in the middle of the Orderly Room, in front of the middle desk of a row of three.

'I'm sorry,' I said, 'but I *didn't* see any evidence of radar equipment. It looked more like a shooting gallery, if you ask me.'

'It's as if—it's as if you have no idea what's going on at all, sir.'

'Let's imagine for a moment that I *don't* know what's going on,' I said. 'Who *were* those people in there!'

'Doctor Jääger?' she said. 'He reports directly to Commandant de la Cour. As does Krzysztof. He's an engineer. He's not billeted with us, you understand, but he works on our vehicles—'

At that moment, Major Edulis entered alone through the adjoining door. I snapped to attention.

'Presumably you have seen this before?' he said, handing me a brown envelope.

I lifted the ungummed flap and retrieved another copy of the aerial photograph. Yet this time the landscape was draped with white annotations, like ectoplasm.

'Commandant de la Cour gave me a copy without explanation, sir. However, I haven't seen these annotations. They are Cyrillic?'

Edulis exhaled sharply through his nose as if balancing the pressure within his skull with the chaos outside it. 'Russian intelligence, which is to say not very intelligent at all. See here, they have labelled the shooting gallery as a radar station, and the block we are presently in is apparently

the canteen for all of the troops they suppose we have garrisoned in the cabins over there.'

'Ah, so that's why Miss Bradshaw referred to the villa as a radar station, sir?'

Miss Bradshaw's eyes wearily described the route of Horus across the skies. Major Edulis continued. 'Your job is to deal with this supposed radar station and its environs, should it be observed again from the air. You see, this photograph found its way into our possession along with certain other plans. Our superiors at present think that they are just a symptom of paranoiac Soviet central planning and unlikely to be used. I wish I were able to be so optimistic. It is just possible they will form the backbone of a Soviet invasion, by sea, along the Essex coast.'

'Sir?'

'The plans describe landing points here,' he said, jabbing the photograph, 'an initial route march, containment of civilians at the Southend bus depot, and cutting off communications between Foulness Island and de la Cour at The Shoe to the south. This would place Foulness Island under siege.' He slid his photograph back into its envelope.

'Hardly a flying start, corporal,' he said bitterly, returning to his office. 'Let's hope you do a better job as a camoufleur. Dismissed.'

The door rattled as he closed it.

The wind clipped my ear as soon as I reached the top of the grass embankment, the villa behind me. The ochre water murmured in the sunlight. A shoal of tiny sanderlings scratched the surface, flashing by turns a collective white belly against the water, then becoming brown—invisible. Kittiwakes and other gulls bobbed like contented buoys, or alighted with the waders that worked the strip of silt recently revealed by the tide, flecked with eroded lumps of wet black masonry.

If they do invade, I thought, *why not just let them waste their time coming out here?*

I took the envelope from my satchel knowing, from bitter experience, that when two or three officers in a row do not know what they want done with a thing, it is inevitable I will have to devise a plan of my own. *They have made me responsible for my own actions; I have lost the only comfort in the chain of command.*

A thin popping sound came from the north, presumably de la Cour's mudlarks performing a munitions test. I twisted my back to the sea, shielding the photograph from a gust, not even close to the whole picture. Yes—this photograph only contains the northeast of the island and a sliver of the southwest. *I need paper and a pencil.*

I head for the nearest shed. The door isn't locked. I remove my coat and hang it up on a coat stand beside the door, empty but for two umbrellas slotted into its base. I make my way down the jetsam valley.

At the far end, I sweep a layer of sand off an old desk's green leather surface. I place the aerial photograph on the desk. I then prise a chair from a tall stack leaning against the wall, brushing more sand and cobwebs off its seat and back. Sitting down, I look at these parallel rows of sheds from the air—if one were to bank them with soil, they would create quite convincing bomb stores. I doubt they're wanted.

In the bottom drawer I find some sheets of thin paper, the top sheet dusty and inscribed with spider tracks, but underneath the paper is good. Looking further afield, among some woodworking tools, I find a joiner's pencil and blade. I sharpen the pencil and take it with the paper and my photograph back to the door, where the small windows have been positioned either side. Holding the photograph against the glass with blank paper on top, the sunlight enables me to trace a copy with the pencil, while the popping sounds from the firing range transmit up the graphite to my fingertips. I return to the desk and sit down, putting my tracing down alongside the photograph.

I look at the two images and consider, as a starting point, that at some time in the past the Soviets conducted this aerial reconnaissance and drew certain erroneous conclusions. What I must do now is make subtle changes on the ground so that, if they were ever to photograph it again, it would tell them a story in two frames. Like those paper discs with a cage printed on one side and a bird on the other. But what story should I tell these Muscovite apparatchiks? That this area is better defended than it really is? That it is abandoned and not worth bothering with? *Oh law*, I feel tired out. Yet the brain is a creature of habit and I will see possibilities.

The difficulty will be to avoid accidentally revealing things to the air that are currently hidden from view. Buildings associated with the hypodermic building in the southwest, for example, its purpose, as yet, unknown to me.

I can see why the enemy assumes there is an early warning radar station here. Part of the Chain Home system. Foulness Island would plug a perceived hole in the Rotor radar defence grid, with Rye to the south, Bawdsey to the north, linking up Chain Home Operational. This assumption can be built on. Radar structures are simple to fake, at least. The gabled barracks already suggest a disguised entrance to support buildings below the surface. Yes—a bunker with a disguised entrance. Something small built in the vernacular style to satisfy the busybodies at the Planning Commission.

Tired out, I feel a burst of irritation; *I shall complain to Colonel Gregory.* I reach for a fresh sheet of paper from the drawer. Perhaps, instead, I will first write a report describing Major Edulis' disobliging reception? Or how Commandant de la Cour detained me for the best part of an afternoon, told me precisely nothing, and embroiled me in personal disputes between himself and his subordinates? The pencil hovers over the paper. *Just tired out. Where was I?* I return to the photograph.

If it isn't tiredness, strange surroundings equally could have unsettled me. More accurately, the human brain is a creature of memory. I sit back and calm myself, marvelling at how details learned by rote will float to the surface: [Earthworks may be sculpted to suggest the displacement of an underground bunker. Twenty-two, or sixty-five feet deep. Two and a quarter inches of concrete. Or three and five sixteenths of earth. Or twelve sixteenths of steel, halving a dose of rads.] *Rote-or radar, ha ha!* That was the idea—a bunker. That might work. I could suggest Foulness Island is the missing link in the Chain Home radar system.

Bunkers are mausoleums for the living. They bury the workers alive in them so they will arrive in the afterlife. *Life after life.* [Corridors should be staggered and capped with steel doors.] *Staggering corridors catch splinters below decks. Chain Home. Rotor. Radar. Rotor. Radar.*

I rub my eyes. Maybe planning can wait till tomorrow. *Any other obvious schemes? Mausoleums? Oh dear, I'm beginning to think like de la Cour!* I feel another burst of irritation at the thought of de la Cour. *I certainly shall complain to Colonel Gregory. Detained the best part of the afternoon!* 'Any other obvious schemes?' I say out loud.

The human brain is nothing like a library. It is more like an ocean that casts things up. [Y-shaped aprons. V-bombers. Hard-standing.] Yes, an airfield. Between Wattisham and Stansted to the north and Manston to the south, one might expect an airfield hereabouts. If we cover these cabins in pairs, roughly eighty feet long, they'd approximate magazine igloos. I'll have to pace them out. A small caravan near the road which could be, at a stretch, an airstrip. Phantom bomber crews sitting ready in their flight suits, reading

the papers, making cups of tea and eating biscuits. *Readiness.* Facing the inside of the hangar doors with cold water running through their flight suits like cold blood. *I wonder what runs through their minds when they're sat there with the engine ticking over? Now, now or now. Now!* Now then ... *Until they stand down and flick off all the little switches. Rotor. Radar. Rotor radar.*

A bomb store is better. *But I shall complain to Gregory first thing tomorrow; look here, Gregory, this really is the limit.* Yes. Yes, a bomb store. I'll make the best of it. Do something simple like adapting these sheds. Adaptation is the word. *Find a niche, adapt, survive. Leave.*

I rub my eyes. I feel a lot better already, having alighted on a plan. The brain feeds on intangible irritations and rewards. Planning is the fun part. The barracks, for example, could be made to look like a fuzing shed for inspecting and arming cores. *I can see the white-coated men penetrating their giant coma patients with x-rays, searching for tiny cracks in their high-explosive lenses.* The paths at either end look like a clearway already, some white gravel would pick them out. *The Russians will imagine the men in white coats rolling the casings in on a sling for their medical.* I remember the mounded stores at Finningley, with an assembly building between the bomb stores and the fuzing shed, *a barrow big enough for two ten-thousand-pound atomic bombs to sleep like ancient kings, ready to wake if their people call on them.* The admin quad in the middle of the site will appear to be a base for Yankee personnel. *Weather-Geats guarding their own ships, enjoying Hrothgar's hospitality, shunning Hrothgar's lookout, guarding Hrothgar's Hall. I suppose that says it all.* I yawn. What I really need is a strong cup of tea.

[Ten.] *Ten years?* That's a staggering thought. Ten years since the War, things have changed. We were just lads, then, cycling down country lanes in the dark. I miss the lads. [Bird.] I miss the camaraderie. I remember making that riverbend in a field. Lighting decoy fires to draw the Luftwaffe away from the city. [Cage.] And when the bombs began to fall, we pedalled like buggery back to our billet, or that blacked-out pub where the landlord kept a lock-in and he wouldn't always make us pay. *The Ministry. Gregory.* [Cage.]

I lift my head up with a start, was I nodding off? *Look here Gregory, our own house in order. Ideas? Root and branch reform.* I slide a blank sheet to the middle of the desk, my pencil hovers as I try to recall my note for Colonel Gregory. Root and branch? Ideas? No. *Can't remember. Tired out. I must keep my head down. Make a stab at something simple and just clear out. Consider the sparrows. From its barrow. Men in white unlock the blast-proof doors and walk out bombs obedient as cows to slaughter. The bulb, switched on from the outside, paints lemon streaks in the bomb's polished black whale-skin. Parallel salmon twilight streaks reflect the sky, moving as they crane it carefully onto their trolley. And men in grey and green and white head to the fuzing shed, out through the clearway, to marry it with its fissile core. Fissile core, fissile coeur. De la bloody Cour.*

I awake with a jolt and reach for the pencil. I write "de la Cour"—*perhaps this can wait till tomorrow. I should get some shut-eye. But no—I want something concrete before tomorrow, so I'm ready for every eventuality.* I glance at my watch. *This is ridiculous, it's not even seventeen hundred hours.* I take up my pencil and make additions to the tracing of the photograph. The clearway. *If the mounded store must be located here, there is plenty of room to the east for a core hutch.* I draw. *The fissile core's party approach slowly through the East aisle, the bride's side, and glimpse the coma king exhumed from his barrow in a black polished casket.* The firing range could be the fuzing shed. I draw a straight path with my pencil. *Tonight his people need him. Tonight we put his heart back in. Tonight sunlight is truncated by the earth's curvature and is failing. The air is groggy. Tonight we make it pulse.* I cross out the barracks. I yawn. I need hot sweet tea and a biscuit. *It's not even seventeen hundred hours! I suppose—I was up at five, though, and I've never travelled well. The man in white, at the head of the procession to the fuzing shed,*

what is he saying? "There will be a new sun over Petrograd, a second sun a little too close, a short-lived blue dwarf hanging over Petrograd, they shall not escape, like a thief in the night, descending from heaven, with a shout, the dead shall rise first, them that remain shall be caught up together with them in the clouds, to meet Him in the air, and so shall we ever be. Comfort each other with these words."

Answer. "We want a king to rule us and lead us in battle."

Priest. "When the storm breaks, where will the grey-green Weather-Geats go?" I lift my head with a start. The bunker entrance. I pick up my pencil. I—*They will run below decks to escape the siren's screeching, there to ride it out. They pound the concrete steps, pass the hot box, and take shelter behind steel shutters. The soil turns to water. Their vessel engraves its underside on the wringing gravel bed. The screeching hull's crazed aggregate sealed with a bituminous damp proof course. Blast and heat. Shock and pulse. They come to rest in a different world. A hundred and fifty days will pass. The war room throngs like a stock-market floor, fallout spume gloams its way on the wind, on the wall, moved by telephone bids.* [Bird.] *A swallow darts through the regional centre of government. The Thegns grow restless* [Cage.] *They look to the Junior Cabinet Minister, the Ealdorman running out of rings to give, until he sends out a raven. The radiation is receding, but the doves drop dead.* "Fling open the steel doors—now!" *Into what?*

"There will always be funerals," the Ealdorman is saying. "As long as the earth endures. Seedtime and harvest. Cold and heat. Summer and winter. Day and night will never cease."

The thing with empty words is they leave room to put your hopes in. Not since churches were so many buildings built to be read from the air. [Gregory! Are we toning down with Novolaut or picking out with Eternite cement? Make up your bloody mind!] *I'll make this point to Gregory. No. Consider the sparrows. Swallows. Rotor. Radar. Rotor radar. Bomb store, bomb store, bomb, store, barrow bird and cage, bird and cage, bird, cage, bird, cage, bird, cage—then, now, then, now, then, now, now, now, now!* then—then I suppose that says it—

Baudelaire's "Recueillement" x 2

Be good, O my Sorrow, calm down.

Be wise, oh my sorrow, and keep yourself more calm.

You wanted Evening; here it comes; it's here.

You clamored for evening; see, it's falling; here it is:

A dark atmosphere enfolds the town,

A gloomy atmosphere envelops the entire town;

Brings peace to some, to others care.

To some it carries peace, to others care and worry.

While the vile multitude of mortals

While among the mortals the vile multitude,

Under the whip of Pleasure, that merciless butcher,

under the lash of Pleasure, hangman without mercy,

Sets out to gather remorse in slavish revels,

goes to reap remorse in the servile feast,

My Sorrow, give me your hand; let's go over here,

oh my sorrow, give to me your hand, come here,

Away from them. See where the defunct Years lean

Far from them. See the late years leaning down,

On the balconies of the sky, in superannuated gowns;

From balconies of sky, dressed in antique robes;

Where Regret leaps up from the depths of the waters, smiling;

See smiling Regret rising from the depths;

Where, under an arch, the moribund sun sleeps sound,

The dying Sun falling asleep beneath an arch,

And líke, drágging from the Eást, a lóng shróud,

And, like a long shroud trailing to the East,

Listen, darling, listen, to the sweet Night coming.

Hear, my dear one, hear the footfalls of sweet night.

LATIN

Latin is the lesson we were taught
Antiquity still living in a "dead" language
I grew up with it as the language of the Church
Made sense of it with the help of a little book, a "missal"
As the priest intoned.
Later, I learned Caesar, Virgil
The long vowels rising up in the deep cadence of the line
Arma Virumque Cano
The labor it was to found Rome
All that history embodied in sounds
Dido mad and loving
The soldier turning away from passion
Carthago delenda est
Rome
Founded,
Rome,
The home of the Catholic Church
The home of a history I had no part of
But which somehow defined me.
The arguments of theologians,
The Church Triumphant,
Heavenly City/Earthly City
Passion, triumph
Perhaps the last gasp of Spirit
Carthago delenda est
How do we become
Most blessed?
How are we
Sanctified in this scramble?
Is renunciation the answer?
Forgive me, father
Mea culpa
Mea maxima culpa
My sins are unknown except to thee
My tears

My history of ill.
In the last hour
Give me strength
To let it all go
To let me die
Like a language
Unspoken
For centuries
Like Latin
Like the Rome of Virgil
Like Carthage
Like, soon perhaps, the Catholic Church
In the vast ruin
Of historical circumstance
And the whirl
Of Time—

when sleep comes
sleep comes
if it comes
until
when sleep comes
until
dream
as we live our lives
or dreamless
day by day
gain new strength
that follows us
when sleep comes
abyss
set mind free
ocean of darkness
(if it comes)
drift
drift
set mind free
ocean of darkness
when sleep comes

abyss
    gain new strength
that follows us
    or dreamless
day by day
    dream
as we live our lives
    when sleep comes
until
    if it comes
until
    when sleep comes

sleep comes

In the amazing
Passage
From the dark
To the dark
We discover
Nothing but life
How did we ever
Get so old?
Springs & summers
Winters & falls
Pass by
As we watch
And learn:
Evanescence,
Mindfulness,
Love.
Evanescence,
Mindfulness,
Love.

    —Mr. Death, he comes knocking at the door.

Paolo Albani

The Post Office Box

Translated by Paolo Pergola—Original title: "La casella postale". Published in Italy in *I sogni di un digiunatore e altre instabili visioni*, Exòrma, Roma, 2018

I have a Post Office box at the Central Post Office in Pistoia, in via Roma.

It's PO box number 313. Someone pointed out to me that it's the license plate number of Donald Duck's car.

I find it convenient to have a PO box because when I didn't have one and I wasn't at home, what happened was that the postman had the bad habit of leaving my mail at my doorstep. As a consequence, in case of rain, I regularly found the mail wet, or, even worse, he would slip it, all crumpled up, in the crack between the two front doors.

None of this has happened anymore, from the moment I got my PO box. If I receive parcels or large envelopes, the Post Office clerk leaves me a note, usually a yellow card, and I collect the mail whenever I want. Most importantly, it's not wrinkled or ruined by the rain.

Therefore, I'm glad I have a PO box. It's too bad that couriers don't deliver packages to PO boxes, which would be a great convenience since the Post Office in Pistoia is open from 8:20 a.m. to 7:05 p.m. and the couriers would have no delivery problems. Instead, every time I order books or other products, I am forced to stay at home, waiting for the courier to arrive, which is a nuisance (the tracking of the shipment does not give you the time of delivery).

At any rate, I just can't stress enough how having a PO box is a great convenience, even if it costs me a fee (years ago, the rental of a PO box was free).

Every day, or almost every day, I pay a visit to the Post Office since it's not far from my house.

This morning, when I got there, a strange thing happened which I didn't expect. I was stunned; I almost couldn't believe my eyes.

I open the box and lean down slightly to see if anything has arrived. Inside, instead of the usual envelopes, free books, bills or stuff like that, I see a guy, a skinny guy, long brown hair and a barely hinted beard, who is lying on the bottom of my mailbox. He's wearing a light-blue cotton shirt with short sleeves. I see him from behind, with his jeans pulled down to his knees, screwing a black girl, a beautiful girl with typical African braids.

The girl has her eyes closed and doesn't notice me.

—Hey, guys, sorry—I tell them—this is kind of my mailbox. What the fuck are you doing in here?

The two don't seem to care, they keep screwing as if I hadn't said a thing.

I don't have the guts to reach into my mailbox (measuring 4 x 5 x 16 inches) and touch the guy's back with my finger or tap him on the shoulder, to warn him of my presence. I'm embarrassed. I don't know what to do. They screw like crazy. I restrain from interrupting their erotic game, although it's taking place, without my knowledge, inside the rectangular space of my mailbox. This, as far as I know, is not a public space, but has other functions related to non-carnal types of communication.

—Sorry guys—I insist, raising my voice a little to make myself heard—can you stop for a moment, please?

At this point the girl opens her eyes and lets out a startled cry, more of surprise and annoyance at the sudden interruption rather than the real anger of an indignant person.

—Hey—the girl says to me as she quickly recomposes herself—what are you doing, watching? you dirty old man!

In the meantime, the guy has turned towards the opening of the PO box, pulled up his jeans and looks at me with a pissed-off expression, the grim look of a thug.

—No, no, wait a minute—I say—I'm not a freakin' voyeur. I'm the owner, that is, the tenant, of this PO box and I was just checking to see if there was mail for me.

—Yeah, sure—says the guy—to check the mail? Sure, sure. I don't think so, I think you were spying on us while we were making love. Who knows how long you've been there for, you son of a bitch!

—No, look, there is a misunderstanding . . .—I stammer.

—Do we know each other?—the guy interrupts me.

—I don't think so—I reply.

—Then you should call me Sir.

This whole story is taking a bad turn.

Unfortunately there is nobody in the PO box room. I have no witnesses to appeal to, so I can't report the two intruders who have taken possession of my mailbox to do their dirty business and fornicate. I could just let it go, slam the flap of the mailbox in their faces and lock them in. However, the fact remains that the box is open in the back by the mail sorting office and the two of them could easily slip out and get away with it.

I don't want them to have it their way.

—Listen dear friend—I resume in an attempt to calm him down.

—Dear friend, my ass—the bully says. He is now standing in my mailbox, his hands on his hips in an aggressive, defiant stance.

—OK, I apologize. I just wanted to tell you, Sir, if you have the patience to listen to me, that there's no need to get angry. I come here most days to

check my mail and to tell the truth I never noticed you before.

The bully keeps staring at me with a strange look on this face but seems almost willing to have a reasonable conversation.

—We've been here for at least three months—he says without losing his contemptuous tone.

Three months?—I ask.

—Yes, three months—he replies.

—If we have never met, it must be by coincidence—continues the bully, and, throwing a mocking smile at his partner, adds:—The other day, just for fun, we pissed on a postcard of yours. It was bothering us, it hindered our movements.

And they burst out laughing, the assholes, doubling over.

Pissing on my mail, big deal, must have been satisfying.

In fact, now that I think about it, some time ago I found a postcard from my friend Franco Giovanetti, sent from Belluno. The postcard had a photo of Dino Buzzati printed on one side, where the writer from Belluno was looking down sadly and had a black hat on his head. It seemed a bit damp, soggy, but then and there I blamed the rain. It had been a period of heavy rain, and I thought the postcard had gotten wet due to the post office's carelessness.

The detail of the discovery of the "wet" postcard and finding out how it got wet piss me off. I can't take it anymore. I lose my patience and burst out:

—You know what? Go fuck yourselves, you assholes!—and I slam the door of my mailbox without even bothering to turn the key in the lock.

I storm out of the room. Without realizing it, I almost crash into a woman with a baby in a stroller. I'm mad. I head towards the post office entrance. I ask for the manager. He receives me immediately. He seems nice. He tells me to sit and after hearing my grievances about the story of the two fuckers who are having a good time in my mailbox, he gets up and closes the office door so that no one can hear us.

Speaking quietly, the director tells me that he is mortified. He apologizes on behalf of the Italian Post Office for the inconvenience I have suffered and informs me that I am not the only "user of numbered PO boxes for lease" (that's exactly how he phrased it, the bureaucrat) to have complained about these illegal behaviors. He informs me that the scourge of the people who illegally occupy the post office boxes—mostly young stragglers, migrants, precarious workers, tramps, but also some retirees who can't make ends meet—is spreading in a worrying way throughout the nation. And anyway, the director adds, keeping his voice down, you don't have to worry because the Italian Post Office has already taken measures, they have drawn up an emergency plan in collaboration with the Ministry of Economic Development and the Ministry of the Interior. Don't you worry, the problem will be solved in a few months.

Aug Stone

Black & White & Red All Over

When Ustin Zamok was but a boy his Uncle Illya taught him to play chess by the firelight of the family dacha. During his second-ever game, Ustin picked up a pawn to advance it to c4 before deciding better of the move and returning it to its original square. His uncle went ballistic. Throwing the chess board into the fire, he ranted and raved about how this is the one thing you never do. "You place that where you originally intended to and I will take your knight!" Little Usy sat there in the oversized armchair listening, his face growing progressively redder through the interplay of shame and the heat of burning rooks, watching as his uncle's great beard punctuated his pronouncements until he had to be physically removed from the room by his brothers. Ustin followed the men out and calmly stated his next move to his uncle, Queen to f5, following on from his previously supposed blunder, but now with a mate in three moves. You learn quickly when the board is on fire.

Despite the intensity of the evening, Ustin did not cry, he swore revenge. And in a most spectacular way. It would be some years before he faced his uncle again over the 64 squares but when the time came he would be ready. Since puberty, Usy, still known by his diminutive, had started growing his own moustache and by the age of 17 it was quite sweeping. The family doctor put it down to a combination of genes and the boy's love of beets. Pickled, roasted, in latkes, shred into slaw, sliced on sandwiches, and of course heavy on the borscht, both hot and cold. And when finished with these scrumptious delicacies, his lower facial features dyed that particular brand of deep red, Usy would delight in working the juices further into his skin with his fingertips, the after-meal effect looking like he'd suddenly been electrocuted whilst simultaneously applying lipstick and rouge. Indeed, if glam rock had existed in the latter part of the 19th century, Usy Zamok would have been among the first picking up an electric guitar. And it was these, the hair-embellishing nutrients and minerals found in the beetroot extract, that the medical man credited the alarming rate at which Usy's moustache was elongating. And for Usy, it was only after such massagings of upper lip that he would reach for a napkin, and of course another, and another, to wipe not face but hands clean. He did not want furry paws, for the same reason he always kept his fingernails trimmed low—lest any part of his hand touch a chess piece unawares. But what worried physician and family was the way in which Usy would consume his beets, his food, indeed, do anything. He had a wild competitive streak that nothing, not even beet juice, could douse. Although they did not know Usy's extended moustache was privately a direct challenge to his Uncle Illya's beard, growing his longer and from less facial space, his family did realize there was something antagonistic about it, sensed his need to have the most bountiful moustache in the area, probably in the world. He was like this with everything. When Usy found out the great Serbian inventor Nikola Tesla used 18 napkins per meal, Usy immediately began requiring 21 such linens to accompany him at table. Though he made a show of using each and every one of them to wipe his hands and the corners of his mouth, there was nothing compulsive about his cleaning. It was simply that Usy knew Tesla had a rule about his dining apparati being divisible by three, and reasoned that if he used anything less than the next multiple up, Tesla might decline to acknowledge it.

Nowhere was his competitive streak seen more vividly than over the chess board. Reasoning that attack was the best form of attack, in every game Usy very quickly went on the warpath. Indeed he would often decorate his face with beet juice before a match, in the style of the native North American tribes he had read about in St. Petersburg's vast library, a favorite symbol being the zigzag across his forehead, representing the lightning that would add power and speed to his play. This lasted until 1901, when all such face paint was banned from tournament play. Meanwhile, he had learned to put his lengthy moustache to another use besides simply show. Leading some to conjecture that he was overly found of the letters 'b' and 'e', though perhaps not of existence itself, using beeswax, Usy would shape the ends of his tasche into loops sturdy enough to lift and convey a chess piece across the board. It was armed with two of these that he was ready to face his uncle again. Illya had not put in much time during the intervening years, playing, yes, but studying the game hardly at all. Usy, of course, had done little else, except eat beets. The rematch was no contest. Usy taunted his uncle every step of the way, letting his lip locks hover over, say, a bishop and then, with a flick of his head, deciding to move a rook instead. Or encircling a pawn with this cyclone of hair, all the while holding his uncle's gaze, and repeating the words 'not touching'. Once in fact purposely grazing the horse's mane of the knight, while simultaneously having his hand swoop in to guide it on its L-shaped journey kingwards. And with a final flourish, declaring checkmate after 21 moves, Usy swept the board with his whiskers to send all his uncle's pieces flying into the awaiting flames of the tableside fire.

It is not unusual for chess masters to have unusual habits, but still Usy's eccentricities loomed large, helping to make him the man to beat. And doing so became the obsession of one Igor 'Igly' Leonov. To Igly, who had lost to Zamok two years before and knew himself to be the far inferior player, it was a matter of psychological warfare rather than any sort of skill at the game. In fact, chess itself was simply the playing field of a much more interior battle, which, if timed correctly, would complete its process of psychic dissolution at the exact moment Zamok noticed his king would be mated. Igly played well enough to qualify for the 1906 tournament in Chernobyl, arriving in the city with facial hair whose length was rivaled only by Usy's own locks, and, along with the rest of his scalp, dyed a deep shade of black. Not a color that would arouse any suspicion, yet Leonov's motives were to align himself with the immense energy of the city and its surrounding area, 'Chernobyl' of course meaning 'black grass'.

It was Usy's habit to arrive early at any such competitions, giving him the chance to go over the room with a keen eye, making sure his opponents hadn't laid any traps for him. He had never got over that initial surprise of his uncle suddenly sweeping a perfectly good chess board into the fire. Once satisfied with these precursory checks, he would make his way around the local vegetable vendors to secure supplies for his stay. He of course traveled with just such a bounty, but besides desiring freshness, he was also curious about what beet conglomerations might then be in vogue in each particular section of the country he visited. He would then spend his time snacking upon such treats until making a final round of preliminary inspections before the start of the tournament. His usual routine this fine Spring morning was set somewhat off-kilter by the contents of the mail he received upon checking in to his hotel. Fan letters were by no means unusual—detailed fantasies of what mysterious members of the public

would like to do to or with his luscious locks, scientific studies of what the senders termed 'criminally ignored' alternative varieties of root vegetable, some postcards commending him on his chess play—but what stood out was a brown paper parcel with no return address, and a forged postmark, though this Usy did not notice, hand-delivered by a gentlemen this morning, though of this the hotel clerk was unawares, as a colleague now finished with his shift had taken reception of the, what turned out to be, book. Strolling to his room, Usy tore off the wrapping and then raised his eyebrows. The accompanying letter proclaimed this to be a recently discovered work of the great Russian master, published privately in accordance with his wishes upon his death—Gogol's *We Got The Beet*. The letter was signed with an illegible scribble but Usy's interest was piqued. He made his way to scrutinize the tournament tables with the hefty volume under his arm.

Igor Leonov turned his face back around the corner from which he had been watching, smiling to himself. The mind games had begun. He continued to follow Usy at a distance, delighting in the master's perusal of the ersatz edition. Indeed Usy seemed positively absorbed by the book as, with his safety checks completed, he sat devouring both it and a copious amount of beet tartare. Igly knew the man to be hypervigilant, and even with being so engrossed in the tome as he was, Usy would not fail to notice, and begin to be unnerved by, the puzzled stares of passersby. With any luck, that was not yet to happen on this first day, a stranger might question the validity of Usy's reading material, causing the latter to become distressed by his own explanations. But there were other matters to deal with even if this did not to come to pass.

As spectators and players alike entered the hall, Usy had for quite some time now been engrossed in Petrovich's quest to secure textile dyes from the Prizrak beet farm whilst simultaneously planning to take over that concern and expand his business to include the manufacturing of his own brand of molasses. Sticky stuff. He barely glanced up from the pages as tournament favorite, the Italian Antonioni, strolled in followed by Geneva's Hadron, another player likely to go far this competition. But with the room almost full, Usy's intuitive senses pricked up when the doors opened upon a confident Igly pausing to take in the scene.

"Imposter!" Usy jumped from his seat aghast, gesticulating wildly to the arbiter. "Bar that man!" Igly Leonov indulged a small smile as he made his way into the room amidst such an eruption. He was off to a strong start.

Usy busied himself passionately explaining to the referee that he had seen this very contestant lose ignobly seven months before in Chelyabinsk and that Igly had had the cleanest face he had ever laid eyes on. Skin of alabaster so shiny, it was barely conceivable that hair could poke its way through. There was no way this charlatan could have grown a moustache to such a scale in only 200 odd days. The hair, he insisted, must be fake. It took some time for the governing committee to make Usy understand that there were currently no rules against playing with a false beard.

Sitting down over the board, Igly, with the luck of the regional color, was playing black. And so had every opportunity to mirror his opponent's moves. Of course any good chess player can dismantle this strategy quickly, but Usy was not himself, unnerved by everything that had occurred with Leonov already. The sight of this man, yes, but on a much subtler level, and one he couldn't possibly know was the work of this adversary, by what Usy had been reading in *We Got The Beet*. The exploits of the two scientists, Fyodor and Nikolai, each the double of the other, working so assiduously on Prizrak's farm. Nikolai tending to the roots from a subterranean lab while Fyodor followed him everywhere, taking copious notes of such experiments, hoping to publish should these undertakings to revolutionize the beet field, in every sense of the word, prove successful. But whose name would go on the final paper? It was not at all clear, especially as the two men's personas began to merge ever further together. There was a strong possibility that Prizrak, as financier, might step in and claim credit, or even Petrovich, who was working furtively with the famed Dr. Dreysky. Usy kept catching himself wondering how it would all play out, and if this could facilitate a real-world transformation of beets as we know them. Already he was beginning to crack. He began periodically placing his hands in front of his face, like a child when it does not want to be seen. Igly of course began doing the same.

Full of his own self-worth, Usy did not much bother with learning the names of his competitors. He knew their souls as expressed through tormented eyes during the throes of a game, what hidden, unspeakable, darknesses lay there that, by their very nature, could not be put into words so easily. When interlocutors could not understand the strange utterances he gave when trying to capture this essence in order to refer to this or that player, Usy resorted to attempting to translate these into a sort of pantomime, which did not make things much clearer. This is all by way of saying that Ustin Zamok may not have been aware that Igor

Leonov was known by most as 'Igly', which of course means 'needles'. Igly himself, who had studied the man thoroughly before this meeting in Chernobyl, was aware that there was a strong chance the master might not know his name, but sat twisting the ends of his great moustache into the finest tips he could anyways, as if to focus some dark magic across the board. Usy held his hands out further away from his face, as if channeling the vision of future celebrities shouting 'no photos please!' as they made their way through a suffocating crowd full of cameras and press. Play adjourned at 10pm, Usy at the point of collapse.

Igly strode in the next day chomping down on a raw beet. It was very tough to chew but the effort was worth it as he watched the blood vessels in Usy's face and neck rush to the skin to match the vegetable's color. Although Usy knew he did not have any whole raw beets in his vast store of snacks, he insisted on calling a delay to the game until he could return to his hotel room and verify that Igly, "or one of his minions", had not "ransacked" his supply while he was away. The much put-upon arbiter agreed; he had dealt with Zamok before. As Usy knew his possessions so well, this did not take very long, and he soon returned to the hall, albeit still steaming. Igly sat calmly in front of the board, continuing to take reverberating bites of his beet. As the heavy crunch of such mastications echoed through the otherwise silent hall, Usy grew weary, shouting from the doorway, "Don't you see?! He's trying to absorb my prowess."

Usy won the first game, but barely. Igly knew it was going to be a difficult path to victory, but he was determined to hang in there. Igly's coach began passing him what Usy immediately identified as beet chips and stopped play to have these inspected. There were no secret messages written on them as suspected, Usy even running his fingers along the one Igly had just received to check for any braille or similarly encoded language that could be read by the tongue. Igly knew how to force his hand. After he consumed the comestible, he made a show of chewing it quickly and then settling in to play faster, even somewhat erratically, as if the chips had been drugged. Sensing this, Usy again halted play and asked for the chips and all Leonov's foodstuffs to be confiscated and sent to a laboratory to be checked for stimulants or any of the mind-altering substances of China and South America that sometimes bestow on the nibbler tremendous visions. In a moment of great vulnerability, he leaned across the table and asked Igly, "how can you sully the beet so?" This match, and the next, ended in stalemate. And as play was speeding up now, Igly feigning being under the influence while Usy grew ever more erratic in his responses, Igly managed a quick victory in the fourth game.

With it all tied up now, the next win would decide who moves ahead in the tournament. As the event sprung into life on this third day, for the first time in his career, Usy had not been the first to arrive at the hall. Instead of studying or getting a restorative night's sleep, he had stayed up late into the small hours finishing the 888 pages of what purported itself to be Gogol's lost masterpiece. Only once he had closed its thick cover with a whimsical sigh did he allow himself to sink into dreams, visions of sugar beets dancing in his head, inaugurating a bright future for all. These fantasies buoyed him through the morning as he dressed and sat down to a beet omelet and beets on toast.

When he did enter the venue, still well ahead of the game, but already teeming at three-quarters full capacity, abuzz with speculation over the outcome of the board, what Usy saw froze him to his very soul. Sitting so as to directly face him, again at his position behind the black pieces, was Igly, looking well-rested and freshly shaven. Usy made a great mental effort not to give in, but what he would see next would be his undoing.

With five minutes until the doors would close and play begin, five gentlemen dressed all in black made their way into the venue and took seats so as to appear to Usy over Igly's right shoulder. Immediately Usy's eyes shot open seemingly miles high as his nostrils flared to the ends of the earth. The party was arranged in such an order so that the occupant of the innermost chair bore a black moustache extensive enough to rival Usy's own. The man to his right sat thoughtlessly stroking one of similar shade but of a length almost exactly half of his compatriot's walruslike whiskers. And so on. Usy's pupils slowing rolling across this field growing more monstrous by the millimeter, until it came to rest at the gentleman on the far right who possessed what anyone else would consider a perfectly normal moustache. Usy could not stop shaking so great was his rage. He poured himself a large glass of beet juice and began gargling with it, for what purpose no one could be sure. Forcing himself at length to swallow, he could not shake the fact that he appeared to be seeing red. A trick of the juice in the light, perhaps? The hue began to merge with the chess board in front of him as if it were on fire, like one he had seen so many years before. With great effort he steadied himself and played his first move—e4. With a studied nonchalance, Igly rapidly responded with e5. Usy let out a deep bellows of breath and, after some time spent with head down blocking out everything but the board, moved his knight to c3. Again, barely had he made this move than Igly jumped his own knight to f6. Usy feeling some semblance of control now flicked his bishop up to c4. Glancing over his left shoulder, Igly then captured Usy's e4 pawn with his knight. Instead of seeing what move was played, Usy followed Igly's initial gaze and when his eyes hit upon the black-clad gentleman at the end of the facial hair processional, this figure returned his stare with an almost imperceptible smile as he raised his right hand and peeled off his moustache.

The effect on Usy was devastating. Away to the door he flew like a flash. And although those in the hall waited hours, the organizers even eventually sending out a search party, Usy never did return to the hall or the great game of chess. Igly was declared the winner by default, though it would be Antonioni who would go on to sweep this particular Chernobyl tournament.

The tale of disturbed former chess champion Ustin Zamok is not as tragic as it would first appear. Using *We Got The Beet* as a springboard, he began his own experiments, keeping meticulous diary entries in the face of all who were calling him insane, and went on to innovate much in the growth and preparation of his favorite vegetable, founding financially successful lines of distribution, even making his way westward to start again in Germany and then France after the Soviets seized control of his farms in 1918. Igly Leonov may have facilitated a victory at the 1906 Chernobyl tournament, but those who are familiar with the whole of the legend know his success wasn't as clear-cut black and white.

Mariana Sández

Too Much Sky

Translated by Kit Maude—Original title: "Para que no sobre tanto cielo". Published in Argentina in the author's short-story collection *Algunas familias normales* (Zona Borde, 2016)

You show dad the photo and he makes a face. *It came out alright, but you need to improve your framing…* Then Florencia butts in and gets him all flustered, telling him he's being too kind about the photo, to you. Like she's trying to blame you for their forced smiles, which were what really ruined the picture. No matter what it is, every fucking little thing, is your fault. And this is when she's making an effort to be nice. Always asking you how things are going at school and whether you have a girlfriend. She doesn't give a shit.

Their faces do look pinched and distorted, the bodies are too low down, squashed, like they were being pressed against the ground, like they feel the weight of the heavens on their shoulders. All that gray sky up above them . . . *That's right*, she says, always being snarky, *you don't want too much sky in there*. Was it really necessary to say that? Don't they realize that you're still learning? Or do they think that the moment you turn fifteen you'll pick up a camera and turn into Picasso or whoever . . . ?

Now they're arguing again. All because you took a bad photo. Because dad's trying to defend you and Florencia can't help being cruel. What did she mean by that wink? That it doesn't matter or some shit. It does matter, things are never just OK. She must be filling dad's head with everything you do wrong: *You can't leave Nicolás on his own for a moment, he's fifteen and he doesn't know how to do anything for himself, he's immature.* Because you're an idiot . . . It must be horrible for dad to hear her complain all the time *I must be crazy for agreeing to*

live like this, nerves shredded, all the air let out. It's a good phrase. Mom doesn't like it when you use it and she doesn't even know it came from Florencia.

Here we go. She's going to make a show of being offended and storm off. Dad's going to follow her, checking out her legs, eyes fixed on her ass. He'll catch up to her and give her a squeeze, they'll hook up and kiss like high-school kids. You know them too well. It'll be hours before they remember you, that they left you on your own, without the camera they took from you during the fight.

Now the couple of little people have come over to ask you to take a photo with their camera. They must be kidding. Didn't they hear the fight? Weren't they paying attention? Say no, you idiot . . . But they're being so friendly. You won't be able to get out of it. If it doesn't come out well you can take more. Just apologize and that's it. Until they get tired of sitting still waiting for you to get it right. Dad and Florencia don't have the patience for that. They want you to get in all the different parts of the landscape: the palm tree to the side, the sea just as a wave is breaking, them from the chest up, when they're saying *cheese* and have their eyes open. The moment you take it, they split up, they get tired of being together, they can't live with one another. The little people, on the other hand, stick tight together, for sure whispering sweet nothings, you can tell from how they look at each other, the way he holds her hand and she strokes his fingers. The way their feet swing underneath the bench. It's funny the way they don't reach the floor. Like you in primary school. But they must be Florencia's age, about fifteen years younger than your father.

It was amazing how they reacted to the photos. She has a contagious laugh. You laughed so hard tears came to your eyes. They thanked you, they were so grateful for the memento. If you hadn't been here, they wouldn't have been able to be in the same shot together. They didn't complain about there being too much sky or anything. In fact they loved it, they kept saying how they were used to it.

Later you can tell dad that they invited you to play checkers at the hotel bar. They say they like to watch the people coming back from the beach in the evening, still covered in sand with their hair stuck to their faces by the seawater, the kids barefoot or in flip-flops, dragging their towels and boogie boards behind them. Others come out from their hotel rooms fresh from the shower, killing time before heading out. They saw you a few times waiting for your dad *or his wife*: they obviously know she's not your mother. Maybe because she's blond and you have dark hair. Or because she's too young. And if she tries to put her arm around you, you shrug it off. Or from the way you kiss her hello, lips barely touching her cheek.

These little people seem happy because they don't have children, or they didn't bring them along; no third wheels. Dad and Florencia act differently when they're alone to when you're around. You've seen how they are in photos of other vacations: always together, tanned, having fun. You get the rows, the sneers, the slammed doors. The threats to break up. Every weekend it's the same: they argue, she leaves, still complaining, without a backward glance, saying goodbye, or whether she's coming back.

Now they're quarreling again, at night in the hotel room. Florencia is crying because she wants to have a baby. Your dad's voice is muffled, you can't hear exactly what he's saying, but it's something like *no, not another child*. He sounds bitter, like he's choking on his words. Now is when she screams *Of course, it's easy to say no when you already have a kid*, but the pain of knowing that she'll never be a mother will eat her alive . . . Why on earth would they have a baby when they're at their best on their own?

She always comes back but lately, every time a little more so, you feel that maybe one day you'll get there and dad will say something like it's over, she's gone, they're through, enough is enough. Man, you don't want Florencia to leave him, he'll fall apart without a woman by his side. The split from your mother was hard enough.

So, dude, put up with it, make an effort to follow her rules. So they don't get so angry with each other about whatever it is you do. But you're not sure that'll be enough. Hard as you try, something always gets away from you, there's always something. Like the joy missing from the photos, the ones you take and the ones you're in.

So NOW Nicolás has decided to spend the whole vacation with the midgets. When you and his father are making such an effort to be friendly. Things aren't as good between you as they are with them but that's no reason to ignore you. You're family. Guillermo, same as usual, doesn't seem to mind at all, everything's cool: *Fine, whatever you like, champ, go, don't get back too late.* The problem is your hands are tied because you're not the mother; if you were, you'd set him right.

You saw the midgets before, on the journey out, but you didn't tell the woman that because you didn't want to admit that you were watching them at the dock, while they were checking in to the boat. You're not about to tell her how amazed you were to see that her parents were normal height and the way her father treated her like a child. They must have gone to see the young couple off. They waved through the glass, the old man crouched down to his daughter´s height with his hands against the glass. It looked like he wanted to touch her, to stroke her hair. The midget woman put her hands to the glass too, like she was trying to reach through it, she stuck out her tongue and they both laughed and then pretended to read each other's lips. The husband was handing over their passports at the desk. The girl's mother stood next to the father but she was stony-faced, staying out of it, pretty cold compared to him. Maybe the whole performance upset her, she didn't appear to have accepted her daughter for who she was, she seemed embarrassed. It must be hard. Depends on how you look at it, or what you want out of life. Because the father was happy, and the daughter was too.

And you're not going to tell her that afterward, on the boat, you saw her standing on a bench like a child. Her husband was sitting next to her looking up at her like she was a queen. A doll queen. His eyes gleamed like sunbeams. You've never seen anyone look at someone else like that before. Or rather you have, Guillermo when you first met him and during the first few years, before the trouble started. It would be pretty stupid of you to say that you spied on them for the whole trip because you loved what you saw between them. Because it made you nostalgic and you thought that maybe it might inspire you to get back a little of what you were missing. You even had the lovely feeling that maybe this vacation might fix everything.

But you did tell her about yourself. Too much. Later, on the beach, when Nicolás brought them over to our sunshade. What on earth were you thinking spilling your guts about Guillermo and the boy to that woman? It never fails, you fire up the motor mouth and then you regret it later. You want to kill yourself. What if the midgets let slip to Nicolás that you want to get pregnant? The kid will only go and tell his father. That you're trying to put pressure on him but he doesn't want one. That when he refuses to have a child you feel rejected. That sometimes you even try things to get pregnant. That you refuse to be a mother to Nicolás while Guillermo refuses to give you a child of your own. Because he can beg as much as he likes but what does that mean to

you? Why should you care? Fortunately, you asked her to be discreet. She's definitely a good person, so don't worry. There's no point getting your panties in a twist, she'll keep it to herself.

She was the one who started it, when she told you she was two months pregnant. You were right to congratulate her, even though you were dying of envy. In love and pregnant, she couldn't ask for more. She was careful talking about herself, she was shy in the way she told you, she's shy about everything. Extremely sweet. It's early days yet, she said carefully, you don't know for sure until the third month and because of who they are, there's always the worry that there might be some kind of physical issue. But they're thrilled, and it shows.

What about Guillermo's face when the woman came over yesterday to show us the photos that Nicolás took? He obviously invited them over to warm up the icy atmosphere that had settled over our table. Christ, they couldn't stop talking about those bad photos. You barely looked at them. The midgets were dark smudges in the distance. They were so happy to share them, they laughed and laughed. At themselves, at Nicolás, at us. They proposed a toast to the future. The future. Nicolás and Guillermo were acting like idiots, falling over each other, laughing, slapping each other on the back, hugging. The midgets lifting the mood brought them closer.

The problem is you're always being left out: the couple don't like you so much. You tried to get close to her, chatting away about girl stuff, but she's not interested in you because you're not Nicolás' mother, you're not Guille's wife, you don't have a child like they're going to have. You're not even the actress you thought you would be when you started out, when you were just eighteen. And you won't be, experience has shown that leading roles aren't your forte, especially not at your age. I mean it, Florencia, you'd better start getting used to the idea: goodbye top billing, goodbye Broadway. Hello supporting roles: filler, stepmother, girlfriend. Just the one scene in the next play; you kill yourself in the gymnasium and after that you're a body with that pretty face you never knew what to do with, except for swearing back when bastards catcall at you in the street. What else? Guillermo won't even do the paperwork to make you common law partners. It's not even on the table right now.

You pretended to look at the photos from afar, so you wouldn't come off so bad, but you had nothing to say. Too much sky, and that hysterical happiness, it turned your stomach. It just reminded you of the haves and the have-nots. Them and you. Like the midget's father, like her mother. Like the baby she has in her womb. Like Guillermo with Nicolás. Nicolás will get everything. Like Guillermo's eyes when you met him, like his eyes now.

YOU'RE GOING to have to man up, Guille, when you get back from the vacation, no more messing around. Having a kid at fifty, dude . . . Florencia even more intense than she is already; women get more neurotic when they become mothers. Especially first mothers. If it hadn't been for how difficult things got after Nicolás was born, maybe you and Estela would still be together. It's not the kid's fault, but you weren't ready and you didn't know how to handle it. You'd give anything to do it over again . . .

Poor Florencia, she, in contrast, thinks that a bundle of joy is going to solve everything: that you'll fall back in love, that it'll bring Nico, her and you together. If only she knew the strain of bringing up a new-born child: work, exhaustion, frayed nerves. Imagine it Guille, changing diapers at your age, warming up milk bottles, rushing to the emergency room over a bout of colic. Then looking for a school, starting all over again, right back at the beginning of the journey. Until

he gets to Nico's age and he's depressed because one of the dozens of girlfriends he's had before he even turns sixteen has dumped him. If only you could explain to him that it'll be years before he finds a lasting relationship and there'll be ten thousand disappointments along the way. That it's not worth getting all worked up over it, choose your battles. And then teaching him to be careful, to avoid unintended pregnancies, not to smoke when he's still so young, to stop secretly finishing off the dregs of wine and beer bottles. Going to pick him up from parties in the middle of the night. Picture it: you spend the night up with the baby, Florencia out cold, and you have to head out at five in the morning to pick Nico up from a club. He comes back woozy, birds cheeping in a circle around his head, planning on sleeping in until the afternoon, if you please. You trying to keep the baby quiet so it won't wake him up and Florencia pissed because you're trying to protect the teenager. Horrifying.

Until she starts being more affectionate with Nico you can't imagine her as a mother. While she refuses to talk to him, when she does it's to say something mean, it would be a crazy thing to do. Afterward she feels guilty, smothers you with affection, does whatever she can to make you happy but she doesn't understand what you really want. It's actually quite simple: peace for Nico; for him to find with us what he has to go looking for with strangers. Fortunately the dwarves are great, the kid has found some good people. But you can't bear seeing your son scrounging for affection with other people because Florencia and the broken family keep him at arm's length. He's acting more and more like he's being driven out, an outsider. And then come the drugs . . . Enough messing around, old man, it's time to get serious.

Especially because Nico isn't stupid and neither is she. They've seen the way your eyes go blank, they've both told you so. You're absent, your face clouds over as though you were thinking dark thoughts, as though life were getting you down. Florencia got it into her head that you had a terminal disease and you were keeping it from her. No more than a bypass for the moment, was your reply. But the truth is that your hair has turned gray all of a sudden, your skin is dry and a greenish color from the two packs a day you're smoking, you're irritable, forgetful. You have the feeling that life is slipping away from you: but at the same time it's like gum you can't get off your shoe.

Admit it, you're with Florencia because she's young, has a killer body and is great in the sack. And because her career is going to take her far. Most men would give their left nut to spend a night with her. You enjoy her passion, except when it comes to having a child. But everything has its price, Guille, you can't expect to get the body, passion, talent and future without giving anything in return.

When you get back home you'll have to tell her that you're still in love with Estela. Yes, dude. Look her in the eyes and admit it: that's how it is, crazy as it sounds, you're head over heels with your ex, the first, Nico's mother. Obviously you need to find the right way to say it. You can't say, for instance, that if were down to you you'd already be back with the women you left six years ago. And it was the realization of what you lost that allowed in all that cholesterol, arrhythmia, excessive smoking, absent mindedness, sadness. The bypass. Gum stuck to your shoe, keeping you stuck in place, forcing you to deal with the life you've made even if you don't like it any more, even though you regret it. Scraping away at the gunk with a twig . . .

Listen up: it's very important that Florencia never find out you've invited Estela out for coffee, more than once. She was reluctant at first but eventually agreed. She was evasive for the most part but the last time you stroked her hand, she didn't pull away or get all haughty the way she did before. She just asked why you were going on vacation with the girl when you were looking at her all googly-eyed. What's going on, Guille? What are you playing at? You can't get anything by her, she has a sixth sense. You love that about her. You didn't say anything, you just looked down at her freckled breasts, wrinkled a little with time and too much sun, but just so, like everything else about her. She didn't ask anything of you, you agreed to meet again when you got back from the beach and had sorted things out with Florencia.

You haven't dared to tell anyone, only the dwarf when he told you that he was going to have a child, just like you and Florencia. You've never cried in front of anyone before, except when your grandmother died, and you were a lot younger then. Now look at you spilling your guts, letting it all come out with a complete stranger. A nice guy, but a stranger nonetheless. His eyes popped wide when you told him that not only were you not having a child but you were thinking of breaking up. To give Florencia the freedom to start a real family. To give Nicolás a more sincere model. So you can quit smoking and reduce the likelihood of an imminent heart attack. Maybe to try again with Estela.

And along the way see if you can't, while you're still young enough, find something approaching the happiness the dwarf couple have. You could copy them, why not? There's still time make amends and learn to enjoy life again. He just told you to make sure because his wife thinks that Florencia is *already* pregnant. She said that she could see it in her eyes, the way she talked about it, and women know things, they're never wrong.

Suddenly it didn't seem so bad when you said that in that case, well then, you'd have to see. Maybe a new addition really might change things. Maybe you'll have to spend a little longer putting up with photos with far too much sky.

CARL LANDAUER

Assignment in New Haven

I didn't know what I was doing here. All I seem to remember is that I was bagging groceries at the 96th-Street Sloan's when I was summoned by a party comrade to speak to Bruno Guevara, the bigwig of the West Side CPUSA. Bruno was, of course, a woman who had changed her name in the memory of Bruno Zentieff, one of the heroes of the thirties because he was the one original revolutionary who was so insignificant that he was left untouched by the purges. Guevara's surname, though, was original. She had made her own way in Communist circles with a stunning series of articles on the Tennessee Valley Authority, of which "The TVA and False Consciousness" is still required reading. But here I was sitting on a hard wooden chair, looking past her at the "Gus Hall for City Council President" poster.

"I've known him for a long time," she responded. "Anyway, we've decided to establish our own Accuracy in America—but we're not going to waste time trying to identify right-wingers; they identify themselves. You do know that Accuracy in Academia is a Socialist Workers Party front group? But back to our subject, we want you to spend your time spying on Marxist professors."

"You mean to tell you if they are living too bourgeois a life, sneaking around the corner for a croissant?"

"No, no, no. Minor luxuries are essential to the professor of the vanguard—how can one

expect to write authentically about the coming workers' state without a croissant and espresso? What we want you to do is to spy on their teaching. You see, we're worried that we have too many flabby Marxists, and the sure sign is if they use the word 'dialectical' too often—one knows immediately that intellectual tic-tac-toe has replaced revolutionary ardor. The situation is disgraceful. Last week I read a book by one of our fellow travelers at SUNY Binghamton proving that Henry James's *Wings of the Dove* is a Communist text. I've forgotten what Milly Theale's disease was supposed to represent . . . Anyway, your instructions are carefully written down."

After a few days of rummaging used clothing stores on the Upper West Side for academic attire—my real coup was a brown sports coat with Lionel Trilling's name on the pocket—I was in the front organization's office in Madison, Wisconsin, "The Norman Mailer Project." The project, I was told, was engaged in a federally funded effort—translating all of Norman Mailer, with the exception of his occasional pieces, into classical Greek. I don't remember the justification, something about comparative linguistics and the translation process. Anyway, they were halfway through *Armies of the Night* when I was shown my downstairs office, complete with a photograph of myself and Mailer, each wearing boxing gloves—they had thought of everything. The assistant directorship of the project was a training position. I would soon be sent out to an English Department or, if they thought I was really good, to a Department of Comparative Literature.

Days passed rather quickly. I often ate my lunches outside even when the weather was getting colder, but I was instructed to spend at least half of my lunch time in the university bookstore, browsing in the anthropology section. On no account was I to look at the literature section—I would immediately lose my credibility as a literary scholar. Once I was given special instructions to buy a Talking Heads album in a record shop on State Street, the street that leads from the campus to the state capitol building, and then double back to the bookstore, look through the latest copy of *Representations* and return to the office. Those were unusually specific instructions—I knew something was up.

That very afternoon I was given my assignment: the Yale Comparative Literature Department. Norman Hastings, the director of the Mailer project—the only real Mailer scholar in the office, who had written a book on the notion of the double in *The Naked and the Dead*—was very solemn as he gave me my assignment. And I knew his solemnity meant something, that my task was particularly challenging. The remaining days in Madison went extremely fast. All I remember is my going-away party with the vodka left over from May Day, some of which spilled over the three impressive blue volumes of Mailer in Greek I had just been given—I remember pondering why no-one had caught onto the fact that the Mailer project volumes were published by the International Publishers, except with hard covers and better paper.

On the way to New Haven, I visited Bruno Guevara, meeting her in the Hungarian pastry shop kitty-corner from St. John the Divine, to receive a few more words of encouragement and a short lecture on the importance of my work. She was pleased at my obvious comfort with the brioche in front of me; they had done well in Madison and she would report her pleasure back to them. All that lay between me and New Haven was a very familiar Seventh-Avenue IRT ride to midtown and a very unfamiliar train ride into Connecticut. As I stared out at the discarded mattresses and refrigerators along the Conrail tracks, I pondered whether my Madison training would be what I would need at Yale. How much would I have to improvise?

My first course at Yale was a lecture course on Hemingway for the English Department. I soon fell behind my own assignments, so I had to improvise. I know I couldn't be seen anywhere near the Cliffs Notes section of the Yale Co-Op, but staring at me from my opened newspaper was an advertisement for a "Bogart Festival" at the local movie house. Tonight was Hemingway's *To Have and Have Not*, next week's reading assignment— all I had to do was a little shuffling, dream up some rationalization for lecturing on *To Have and Have Not* a week early. In class the next day I experienced a few embarrassing moments, accidentally referring to Bogart. But the embarrassment passed quickly when I remembered that the students hadn't read the assignment yet and wouldn't read it anyway. Besides, they are never surprised when their professors mention characters that they had missed altogether. It was not long before I had purchased a used VCR, one that for some reason introduced television commercials into the films I had rented from around the corner—I still haven't figured out how to turn off the "commercial function."

I designed all my courses to fit Hollywood's products, and it worked like a charm, until my first graduate course. My graduate students noticed that something was wrong when I referred continually to Burt Lancaster's lines that they could find nowhere in John Cheever's "The Swimmer." I knew it wouldn't be long before I would be back in Bruno's office, having failed my assignment, for the news about my film references quickly swept through the department. I was supposed to meet the department chairman for lunch that Friday, and I still remember shaking violently as I paced back and forth in front of Mory's. Finally, I recognized the familiar raincoat of the chairman as he walked up York Street with his quick gait. He approached with a broad smile, "I'm delighted about your new theoretical turn. I want to hear all about it." A Deconstructionist himself, he dominated our lunch discussion with praise for my "collapsing" of literature and film as categories. I had, he assured me over an albino salad, added to the deconstruction of the author as subject. All I needed to do was to put some of it into print.

Almost overnight my "work" became nationally recognized. The *New York Review of Books* was full of debates on the cinematization of literary criticism and "Film-reconstruction." Even *Commentary* devoted an issue of one of their "symposia" to my theoretical turn, asking contributions from all their usual participants (I'm still enraged by William Barrett's snide remarks). The following December I was to give a luncheon address to the Modern Language Association Convention in Chicago on "Filmic Interludes in a Logos-Centric Tradition." I was never able to give the talk because late one night in New Haven I received a call from Bruno. Her voice was nervous: "Everything's off. We've been directed to terminate the whole program. But we are reassigning you to a Contra-infiltration group training near Guerneville, California." So I am sitting now in the woods near the Russian River with a barbell in one hand and a copy of *Soldier of Fortune* on my lap.

Marvin Cohen

Bees, Snow

BUMBLE BEES AND PEOPLE.
YOU CAN PRAY FOR THEM IN A STEEPLE.

Has Evolution earned our gratitude?
That's my earnest attitude.
It's produced the whole damned human race
from barely an earlier trace.
You and I are two of them,
so let's sing an appreciative anthem
to Evolution, that solidified phantom.
Without it, what would we ever be?
Maybe only a bumble bee
that offers pollen to flowers
to while away the May-time hours.
Do the flowers ever accept?
If not, all of Nature will have wept,
and rain pour down with such luster
that flowers will grow up quick in a cluster.
Nature is great, and so is art,
which derives from humanity's being smart
and having a big wide-open heart.
The world will certainly approve
that bumble bees and people are in the groove.

SNOW IS GETTING OUT OF HAND,
AS THE DRIFT PROCEEDS TO EXPAND.
IN DANGER OF SLIPPING, WHO CAN STAND?

Snow is falling at an alarming rate.
Will it make an elaborate city sculpture,
with its consequent disrupture,
of many stalled cars
and buildings and shops?
Tell me when it stops.
Then the town will be allowed to breathe,
and normal traffic proceed.
Commerce is at its height,
but winter snow proclaims a blight
to halt the progress of the usual
on society's hectic procedural.
Snow will enforce a day of leisure.
Streets and avenues are plowed with snow,
and when it stops, only the weatherman will know,
to convey via television
an onward going vision.
But schools are closed, so we're in prison,
and business has to halt,
due to the weather's inclement fault.
Pour on bodies some preservative salt.
Can Spring be far behind
from this violation of the mind?
No, then blossoms will blow
irrelevance on the snow.

KURT LUCHS

THE REMARKABLE YEAR: PHILIP LARKIN LOOKS BACK ON SEX

T.S. Eliot once voiced the opinion that the best poet to write in English in the last 200 years was W.B. Yeats. Although Old Possum was wrong about many things, I believe he was right about that. Which leads us to the follow-up question: Who is the best poet to write in our language since Yeats? We might have to answer that in two parts, depending on which side of the Atlantic Ocean we're talking about (two peoples separated by a common language and all that). In America, I'd say possibly James Wright, possibly W.S. Merwin, possibly Louise Glück. In the U.K., I think it's either Ted Hughes or Philip Larkin, a pair of polar opposites. For my money, Hughes edges out Larkin, but there's no denying the strength and durability of Larkin's achievement.

As one of the primary apostles of formalism, he helped drag rhythm and rhyme kicking and screaming into the latter half of the twentieth century. The trick is always to fit ordinary speech comfortably within formal constraints, with thoughts, images and turns of phrase so arranged as to be meaningful and memorable. Easy peasey! Larkin is a poet of the everyday, seeking illumination in the quotidian. More often than not, he finds what he's seeking. Many of his poems are now justly regarded as classics.

The poem we're looking at today, "Annus Mirabilis," was written in June 1967 and seven years later became part of the final volume published during his lifetime, *High Windows* (1974). In it he looks back nostalgically on the beginnings of the sexual revolution, only a few years old at the time of writing, but it must have seemed like centuries, so vast were the social and cultural changes the decade had wrought. How appropriate that this poem should be one of the first to mention the Beatles, seeing as they had led and come to symbolize those changes (Allen Ginsberg's "Portland Coliseum" from 1965 mentions the group members by name but not the group itself).

I'm guessing it's no accident that the manuscript bears a date of June 16, 1967, exactly three weeks after the release of *Sgt. Pepper's Lonely Hearts Club Band*. That the Beatles were doing work of lasting value had been apparent since at least 1965 to open-minded listeners from the worlds of jazz and classical music, including Miles Davis and Leonard Bernstein, among many others. However, *Sgt. Pepper* was the turning point that caused every culture critic to take them seriously. When Larkin wrote "Annus Mirabilis" he could feel confident that name-checking them would not make the poem seem hopelessly dated someday.

The poem is 20 lines long, consisting of four stanzas of five lines each, employing a rhyme scheme of ABBAB. The meter is mostly iambic, with plenty of exceptions. The first stanza neatly sets the scene:

> Sexual intercourse began
> In nineteen sixty-three
> (Which was rather late for me)—
> Between the end of the *Chatterly* ban
> And the Beatles' first LP.

The trial of Penguin Books under the Obscene Publications Act for publishing the unexpurgated edition of *Lady Chatterly's Lover* by D.H. Lawrence resulted in a "not guilty" verdict on November 2, 1960. That the author's worst book effectively rid Britain of literary censorship is about the only good thing one can say about it. Penguin should have been prosecuted for publishing a misshapen novel that managed to make sex both boring and mawkishly stupid. The Beatles' first album, *Please Please Me*, came out March 23, 1963. Between the two dates singled out by Larkin fell two other events worth noting in regard to the sexual revolution. On December 4, 1961, birth control pills became available through the National Health Service, though until 1967 they were only given to married women. And in the summer of 1963, the Profumo scandal broke open.

That's the backdrop. The only use of first-person in the poem occurs in the parentheses in stanzas one and four, windows into Larkin's own view of these events. Why, one wonders, does he feel that the sexual revolution was "rather late for me"? Because he turned 41 in 1963? Even before the advent of ED drugs, middle-aged people embraced the new sexual ethic as eagerly as the young. More so, perhaps, because they knew all too well what they had missed growing up.

That, in fact, is the subject of stanza two, where he recounts the old order, in which sex is "A sort of bargaining, / A wrangle for a ring, / A shame that started at sixteen / And spread to everything." To sum up the institution of marriage as "A wrangle for a ring" is profoundly dismissive and reductionist. And yet, from the young man's point of view, maybe not so far off. How insightful of Donald Davie to call him a poet of "lowered sights and diminished expectations." Larkin went through a pronounced Auden-worshipping phase when he was learning how to write, and this stanza does display some of Auden's genius for generalization.

Stanza three tells how things have been since the sexual revolution, which quickly produced "A brilliant breaking of the bank, / A quite unlosable game." Happiness all around, it would seem. Yet stanza four concludes the tale almost exactly as it began, on a note of irony mixed with poignant regret:

> So life was never better than
> In nineteen sixty-three
> (Though just too late for me)—
> Between the end of the *Chatterly* ban
> And the Beatles' first LP.

Treating the final stanza like the repetitive chorus of a pop song—shades of the Fab Four again—is a clever touch that drives home the underlying conflicted nature of the poem. If "life was never better," why does he have to keep saying that? Is he consciously echoing the song "Getting Better" from *Sgt. Pepper*, with the chorus that undercuts its own ostensible message, "It's getting better all the time (it can't get no worse)"? Yes, I think so. And here is a good place to leave off our examination of the poem, at the point where Larkin demonstrates that the sexual revolution was part of a bigger cultural tsunami that changed much more than sex, among other things causing high art and pop art to mate, blend into each other and became all but indistinguishable.

KURT LUCHS

1964

They could do no wrong that year, no matter
What they set their hands to, it came out right.
Author Lennon proved mad as a hatter,
They conquered the world with "A Hard Day's Night"
(Movie, album *and* single) and they toured
Every stadium on the globe until
Their desire to play live was almost cured,
Except they still had contracts to fulfill.
The girls, the screams, the comic repartee
Must have blurred together as they rushed from
Studio to studio—BBC,
EMI, United Artists—pushed from
Limousines into humanity's arms
With no protection but their natural charms.

Marc Estrin

Occupy Beethoven's Ninth!

Beethoven's Ninth—not the longest in the symphonic repertoire, nor the loudest, but the hugest in concept and goal.

Unfortunately, for many of us, our knowledge of the work consists of just the tune to the last movement, as sung to various texts around the campfires or in church. Back in 1893, George Bernard Shaw ridiculed a listener who knew only the Ninth's last movement, the "Ode to Joy," and came to hear it only for that. He writes about the poor chap sitting there "bothered and exhausted, wondering how soon the choir will begin to sing those verses . . . and hardly able to believe that the conductor can be serious in keeping the band noodling on for forty-five mortal minutes before the singers get to business."

This is a problem. For the Ninth is a work which wants to tell the largest of all stories, one with a beginning and a middle, and, hopefully, an end. Yet only the end is the part "everybody knows." And this audacious end was questionable even to Beethoven, who continued to make sketches for an instrumental movement, and who, some years after it was finished, remarked that the choral finale was a mistake.

The choral finale has been questionable down through the years, to musicians of Beethoven's generation and beyond. Ludwig Spohr, though now all but forgotten, was a considered major composer of the generation just after Beethoven's. The Choral movement, he thought, was "so monstrous and tasteless and, in its grasp of Schiller's Ode, so trivial that I cannot understand how a genius like Beethoven could have written it."

So I'd like to ask the heretical question: *Should the last movement of the Ninth BE the last movement of the Ninth—or was Beethoven caught up in some extra-musical, utopian thought which has left us with a flawed and freakish masterpiece?*

To help you decide, let me sketch out the big story of *all* the movements, and the personal and historical background out of which they grew.

By 1824, Beethoven had been deaf for two decades, and stone-deaf for the last five or six years. There is a moving story of his "conducting" the premiere of the symphony, beating time and turning the pages of his score even after the work was over. Beethoven was a passionate man whose years of deafness had isolated him and kept him from most human intimacy. His great heart was forced to content itself with visionary goals of brotherhood and civilization. A wife, a family? There was none.

Lacking a happy story of his own, Beethoven was forced into the wider world of cosmos and myth where his lifelong love of Schiller's "Ode to Joy" came into play, and grew into his projection of the end of history, of universal life become universal love. The Ninth was Beethoven's map leading to the home he always wanted but never achieved.

Beethoven's "late period" explores a world completely removed from ordinary thought and experience. His musical technique over the years had evolved beyond the bounds of anything known, before or since, both utilizing and disrupting all elements of classical design. He threw everything he had into the Ninth: Maynard Solomon lists "harmonic and rhythmic motion slowed to the edge of motionlessness, clouded harmonic progressions, passages in indeterminate keys, nebulous and nocturnal effects, multivalent tonal trajectories, enormously extended time spans, highly idiosyncratic fugue styles, and a supremely ornamented variation style that implies the infinite possibilities latent in even the simplest musical materials."

All this, you will hear, beginning at the beginning . . .

First Movement

. . . the *very* beginning, before there is a world. We hear the tremolo of the Cosmos, gestating. E, A, open strings, open fifths, outlining, but not defining, a riddle of what's to come. Beethoven here begins the utmost three-movement exploration of the fundamental components of music: interval/harmony, rhythm, and melody. In the beginning was the open fifth, uncommitted to major or minor emotion, beyond them, primeval, inhuman. At the thirteenth measure, a dark theme emerges from darkness, then falls back, abandoned, but committed. This is a theme which brings up memories of Beethoven's earlier struggles with Fate—for example, the Fifth Symphony's "Fate knocking at the door"—but here evoking a fate beyond personification, beyond defiance. We are present at the creation, and we find it not benevolent, but rather crushing and dissipating, an inhuman beginning to the story that will end (at least tonight) with the brotherhood of Man. The scale, the range, the proportions are gigantic, the potential cataclysmic. In case we, with our current familiarity, are tempted to try to snuggle up against it, we are brutally dismissed by the grinding despair of the funeral march which marks the movement's end. "Beware," it says, "this could go anywhere."

Second Movement

Rhythm is featured here, a demonic dance obsessively thrusting in this, the only second movement scherzo in all the symphonies, still impersonal, as was the first. The orchestra takes off in a *molto vivace* uprising of blind energy, four hundred measures of hang-on-to-your-hat.

But then something very strange happens. Formally, a scherzo requires a trio, a contrasting middle section, before returning to its original intent. What is strange is that the trio is a human one, the sound, perhaps, of a peasants at a dance, a surprise invasion of another universe, at another scale, a hint of benevolence. And if you listen carefully, you will hear in the trio theme the outline of what will become the "Ode to Joy," a beneficent, gratuitous kindness after all the flinging. But it is not time yet for humanity. The scherzo returns, chaotic and hostile as ever. The trio gives one last little try in the winds, but is beaten down by the full orchestra crashing emphatically on an open D chord, neither major nor minor. Case closed—but open. Rhythm, for all its beating of drums, cannot be the essential mode of humanity.

Third Movement

Melody. Here is the human mode. I am not the only complainer who thinks the symphony culminates, and should have ended, with the Adagio/Andante, who feels that *it* is the work's *true* finale. Such would not have been alien to Beethoven's late sensibility: of the last three piano sonatas, two (op. 109 and 111) end with astounding slow movements. In his *Doktor Faustus*, Thomas Mann has a character consider why Beethoven had not written a normal, fast, last movement to op. 111: "A new approach?" Wendell Kretschmar asks. "A return after this parting—impossible! It had happened that the sonata had come, in the second, enormous movement, to an end, an end without any return." And when he said "the sonata," he meant not only this one in C minor, but the sonata in general, as a species, as traditional art form; it itself was here at an end, brought to its end, it had fulfilled its destiny, reached its goal, beyond which there was no going . . ."

Schiller himself, the poet of the "Ode to Joy," had written "it is through beauty that we arrive at freedom." Beauty. Like the beauty of the third movement. So can the last movement be the arrival? No one has ever contended it was beautiful.

But Beethoven didn't agree. "This is too tender," he remarked of the third movement. He felt he needed to escape a trap of passivity, a beauty too sublime for action. And so he forces us to leave this gorgeous, inward, mystical contemplation, this rich, flowering serenity, these slow, deeply human, personal, miracles, timeless, beyond decay . . .

Fourth Movement

—to be blasted away by the most gargantuan Fart in music, the chord which begins what Wagner called a *Schreckenfanfare* (terrifying!), blowing off not only the sublimity of the previous movement, but all that came before it. The basses and celli start literally talking—but they have no words—we don't understand what they say. Then—are we hearing right?—the symphony starts over again from the beginning—only to be cut off, dismissed by the basses. Next, the scherzo gives a try, again to be dissed, and finally, the slow movement, to be more gently tossed. What is it the basses want? After a pause, they tell us.

The "Ode to Joy" melody, for all the sketches which preceded it, has all the attractiveness of a beer hall tune. But if one wonders, with Spohr, that a genius such as Beethoven could come up with something like it, one's cynicism is dissolved as the master begins spinning out an increasingly complex set of songful variations, growing his sound through strings and winds, and finally punctuating it with brass when, lo, the *Schreckenfanfare* returns, and a solo bass—the first human voice ever heard in a symphony—translates for us what the basses were trying earlier to say: "O friends, not these sounds. Rather, let us strike up something more pleasant and joyful."

What is he talking about—"these sounds"? A little ambiguous. For it is not merely the first three movements that are being dismissed, but necessarily the very "Ode to Joy" theme, which has just received such gorgeous orchestral treatment. It must be non-vocal symphonic music itself Beethoven means, thus calling for the end of yet another genre, as insufficient to attain his goals for the future.

The first response of the collective human voice is "Freude!"—joy—and the chorus basses begin to sing the words to the first Schiller verse. All begins at a natural, human scale, but with each successive development, the music separates itself further and further from normal song, and begins engaging other, less definable levels of experience. The text takes a surreal leap from the pleasures of the worm to the seraphic joy of angels (*Wollust ward dem Wurm gegeben, und der Cherub steht vor Gott*), and we are translated into a new world, in a new, surprising key. We are directed by Beethoven/Schiller to be as heroes, joyfully racing through the heavens to victory, and the orchestra breaks into an enormous fugue with the rhythmic drive of the discarded scherzo, ending in a four-part choral version of the Joy theme, its definitive statement from the billion-voiced throat of humanity.

But now things get really strange. We are exhorted to the world's largest group hug (*Seid umschlungen, Millionen!*). On your knees! Don't you sense the Creator? Look up there. He *must* be there—above the stars. The music goes anti-gravitational.

So we look and listen. And what do we hear? The most bizarre double fugue in the history of music with lines quite unsingable, each making little individual sense, but—as if proving something about community—evoking an undeniable, powerful, visionary gestalt. The energy gathers itself, and the work literally sprints to the finish line, prestissimo, and is over—thrilling, yes, but do you want to live there? We've survived the cold vastness, the kinetic shoving, the opiate beauty of the first three movements. And now?

In the last movement of the Ninth, Beethoven was reaching for some exalted idea of brotherhood in a life sprung from all that preceded it. But I, for one, have always felt disappointed, even tricked. For all the phenomenal musical events in the last movement, theologically, it feels more like some enthusiastic, non-denominational Sunday sermon. OK, OK, this is music, not theology. But finally: is the music of the last movement the fulfillment of the path set up by the first three? Or did Beethoven opt to use his unmatched skill and energy in the service of a politically and psychologically urgent but non-musical exhortation?

There is no decisive conclusion here. The English musicologist Donald Tovey insists that, like it or not, we MUST listen to the Ninth *as if* the chorale finale were correct. Still, one wonders.

Bobby Parrott

My Seismic Bedtime Workhorse Measures Its Luck in a Time-Lapse Garden of Stars

Molecular fretwork pulls in the signal, televises
my motorbike's roller-coaster xylophones
in tandem, and I can only guess it's about love.
I'm drawn by the allure of your leg muscles'

flavorings of astonishment. But can we afford
this sputter of yogic slogans long enough

to elevate your retro-spin clavicle into its stroke
of violoncello? Penetralia aside, all we unplug
is our selves, the viscous longing we hear slicing
moonbeams from trees. There's no gateway

like the mouths of giants for this, or in the less-
kept secret of lavender, my seismic bedtime

workhorse. Short of clandestine, unbroken
love is about how much more the dolphin
of sleep craves our extinction's crash. And yet
in this bumper-car household of elves

we smash portraits on over-greased mantelpieces
to wax more than mechanical. No longer

brides, we magazine fractured god-berries, collect
toadstools, kneel inside a hover of cliffs, melt
in the buzz of tongue-kisses gifted before names
are exchanged or purses looted. Geothermal

boredom your skin's vortices minus the tantric
stammer this precise species of hominids

can unlock. I squirrel blind earthquakes in each
shirt pocket even as my cat purringly returns
my best slow-blink, levitates me toward *my* place
among her flowerbed of mouthwatering stars.

Memory Forms: Ruins

1. Dead Crabs Beyond the Dunes
Seaside, Oregon

Hear the coast crash monotonous
like foam fluttering behind the storm.
It is night now and the red glow of signage
beckons us along streets slick with rainwater
and whatever gets carried along an ocean's surface.

Hear that coast crash mesmerized or mesmerizing.

With a gut of fried fish we hold ourselves up
and stumble along with minimal beams,
flashlights working while the rain works still,
glasses fogging up before fully coated in water.

What greets us beyond the black dunes this evening?

Orange and yellow crabs, thousands of them.
The shells unmoving, the sand and water within unmoving.
I can almost see their faces. I can almost watch their pincers.
I can almost scuttle alongside them back out to sea,
the neon faded out as the watery depths become.

2. "Touch Real Dinosaur Bones"
Dinosaur National Monument, Colorado

Hours later we're staring at long, winding roads
    that just
                    don't stop
                            for us.
Back in the glass cage,
    bones of strange beings
                    stared
                            back.
Calming effect.
    Laced nature.

Turning up the volume
and speaking volumes.

I imagine the gasses of suffocation
and being in this wondrous space
covered in worlds only imaginable.

The Park Service created a taxonomy of experiences
their icons undeniably hip, keeping me from thoughts
of murder and contagion, of disruption and that ceasing echo:
& Plants & Animals
and the recognition of a single leaf
& River Canyons
and the embodiment of oxbows and whitespace
& Ancient Cultures
and representation of thinness and jewelry
& Geology
and the streaks that are simply that: streaks
and striations
& Paleontology
and fullness of teeth, predatory, spooking
& Homesteading
and the simplicity before the struggle, with windows

Touching the dino bones, I drone on and on about
distraction and denying my experience: the norm.

But there is something about history.
Moments within spaces condoning and allowing.
Containers   for containing   this.
Structures   for instructing
in ambience.

To think this is how I feel, thinking back,
along a bumpy road to Echo Canyon,
along a way that can lead
to the next extension.
Meanwhile,
what do the bones think?
What do the collections
feel?

3. Return to Empty
Seattle, Washington

A palace among the dogwood and it trembles.

Beyond the tiger lily an ancient rock.

And its chiseled face bare.

We are ruptured. We are dislodged.

Memories captured, compressed in snow melt.

Sun pushing inward, water pushed toward earth.

Even on this day. Even in this breath.

I can feel this return. I can feel this lingering emptiness.

I feel as the long burn serves missive from the meadows.

A typography of flame reaches out to a withered parchment of skin.

Yes, today. Even today.

The core is blue and it is sustaining and we watch within as we dance through this summer.

Consider bends in light scraping gentian and valerian.

Consider the methodology of escape.

Talus and scree. Here. It's here.

With survival breath accompanying sweat. And now. It's now.

I am inhaling and exhaling. Be it too soon, we are still arriving through breath.

Around a corner: a plunge to reach a sacred bottom.

There are ruins beneath that bring more questions.

Aquatic trauma accompanying divinity.

It extends onward through the shallows, through the dusk.

Forever its linger. Forever I can hear it calling in rush and awe.

Liquid and its green signals and gray patterns.

Submerge meets emerge.

A single trillium withering purple and brown.

There is the glance backward. Memory's zoom.

Back to the bounty and its precedent.

Back to the glacial, an Olympics poem.

Return, over shoulder's creak and creek's hush.

Stone array to elevate the difference.

Of difference. Of loss. Tales of those coming up onto the shores.

Clambering through climate and its migrants holding breaths, holding sighs.

Tiptoes through preservation. Pounces across ravaged remains

Past stances of their former shadows.

When the movement settles, I dream.

I dream in old peaks and past voices. Echoes ongoing or spidery hallucinations.

Those whose bodies gave in and gave us their space.

Talismans of forgotten roads, paths, holding grounds.

I dream in ruinous life and the blanket of limbs in the ruins.

Barely hanging on, barely hearing, barely breathing as it spreads.

Smoke's wisps rolling through the night.

Dawn's facade a grimace and enough.

Pools of blood clotted in yellowing smoke light.

Pools of dried blood glyphic and perpetual.

The vicissitude within a warren. Alive.

Memories of moonlight dictation and commands of survival.

Morphing across realities we continue to open.

Opened eyes after twisted keys, pressing in and finding the next.

In this land of drought and my own ragged, wagging tongue,

dangling like a peace treaty around my chin,

I invite the reemerged in a mess of light.

I dream and I invite languages of breaking and mending.

More clusters, more shapes of us.

Birthing a glance of another sequence.

Come, join us until we crumble.

KURT LUCHS

An Interview with Translator Dasha C. Nisula

Dasha C. Nisula has translated two outstanding collections of poetry by 20th century Croatian poets. The first was *You with Hands More Innocent: Selected Poems of Vesna Parun* (Exile Editions 2019), the second was *Music Is Everything: Selected Poems of Slavko Mihalić* (Exile Editions 2019). The following interview with her was conducted by email in the closing months of 2021.

How did you become a translator? What was the original impetus and how did it progress?

I have been a translator for as long as I can remember, growing up in Chicago in a bilingual home. Navigating between English and Croatian or Russian, translations were initially simple. Once I began working part-time for the Berlitz School of Languages, while working at Northwestern University Medical School, these translations became more complex and demanding. But the impetus to translate poetry came to me at the University of Southern California, where I was working on my graduate degree in Comparative Literature. While studying I was teaching both Croatian and Russian. We had a number of choices for Russian texts; however, there wasn't much of a selection for Croatian. To make classes more interesting I began bringing in some poems by Croatian poets, including those by Vesna Parun. And it was then that I first began to translate Vesna Parun seriously.

Having completed my graduate studies, I moved to Michigan, where at Saginaw Valley State University I began teaching English while continuing to translate poetry by Vesna Parun. I first pub-lished her poems in the *Journal of Croatian Studies*. Then one of the English professors, Mr. Raymond Tyner of Green River Press, offered to publish the first bilingual edition of Vesna Parun's poetry. At the time I thought I could only translate poetry by women and wanted to bring forth some of the neglected talent from Eastern Europe.

Do you write poetry yourself? If so, what has it taught you about translating?

I used to write in my twenties, but working and studying did not offer much time, so I wrote late at night. As I was exposed to excellent Croatian and Russian poets, I realized that there is better talent out there than I can offer. But to introduce these fine poets to the English-speaking world, I thought that would be something I could do. What has helped me as a translator is knowledge of Slavic languages, love of music, and a good ear.

How does a translator decide which poem to translate?

For this question I will reply with something Slavko Mihalić wrote in one of his poems. He says "the poem alone seeks its poet." Having understood that, I came to the conclusion that each poem also seeks its translator. I hold this to be true at least for me, since I have never been able to translate a whole book of poetry cover to cover. I select poems in a collection that speak to me.

There are poems I do not fully understand and, no doubt, there are a number I translated which some may think not very well of. But then it is also important to check the original to see how good the original text is in itself. And that is why it is important to be able to read the language of the original poem and not just improvise or make up a poem based on a few translated words.

Tell me about some instances where a poem defeated your efforts to translate it. Why?

There have been poems I translated that just did not work out well when I read them in a new language. Others were dated for a particular country or time period which is not well known or understood. I simply let them go. This is particularly true of poets writing during a very stressful period in their country's history. My favorite selections have always been poems that speak to all humanity about the human condition.

In addition, there were poems that I had started to translate, but then at the second or third stanza they just did not read right, and at that point I would let them go. It is interesting to note that translation has to be done in multiple attempts, since one day the poem is puzzling, and on the next it makes sense. The same is true in creating an original poem; one goes over the words multiple times and at different times of day.

Who are some of your favorite translators and favorite works that they have brought into English?

I do not have a favorite translator, but I admire all who attempt to open a door to a different language, new ideas and culture. My educational experience in comparative literature required at that time that we read in four languages. I have been exposed to original and translated works from the beginning and learned that every two decades or so a new translator appears, building upon the work of previous translators in that language. The best ones acknowledge consulting works by a previous translator. No doubt all are familiar with the name of Constance Garnett, who brought into English such Russian authors as Dostoevsky, Chekhov and Tolstoy. What we know of her is that she kept close to the original and someone would almost have to consult her translations. And then there were others such as Andrew MacAndrew, Ralph E. Matlaw and, more recently, Richard Pevear and Larissa Volokhonsky, whose works I read and respect.

I read translations by Stanley Kunitz, and those by members of the American Literary Translators Association (ALTA), such as Michael Naydan, who translates from Russian and Ukrainian, Alexis Levitin from Brazilian and Portuguese, Adam Sorkin from Romanian, and Diana Der-Hovanessian, who translates from Armenian. I also enjoy reading translations from around the world that *The Massachusetts Review* regularly brings to English readers.

I'm wondering what role, if any, your own femininity played in translating Vesna Parun?

As a human being and a woman, I think I understand Vesna Parun quite well. Not only that, but her language is clear and direct. In addition, she wrote poetry that was rhythmically freer and contained spontaneous, unrestricted rhyme without formal stanza patterns. She used free verse and colloquial expression that confirmed her strictly personal and unconventional lyrical expression.

Following SVSU I ended up teaching at Western Michigan University and began attending and presenting my work at ALTA conferences. I learned that Elizabeth Bartlett, a recognized poet in her own right, had been working on her third volume of international anthologies published every four years, coinciding with the Olympic Games. She was inviting submissions from translators. I submitted a number of women from East and Central Europe and served as Associate Editor for the Central European section of the anthology. Subsequently I was asked to edit the fourth volume and accepted. In that anthology I also included my translations of numerous women from Russia and countries of former Yugoslavia. I was planning to publish separately an anthology of women poets from Central and East Europe. However, some of the comments I received from the publishers revealed they were not interested in publishing only women.

Then, while participating at a conference on Croatian literature in English translation, organized by Slavko Mihalić, I had a chance to meet him and was given his full collection of poems, along with permission to translate his work. It took a long time due to teaching obligations, but I finally managed to put together a volume that was published by Exile Editions in 2019.

In the meantime, I was also reading journals from Croatia and found a poem there that had been translated into Croatian from Russian. I wanted to translate it into English and contacted the Russian poet Vyacheslav Kupriyanov. Once I obtained his permission to translate, my journey into translating male poets was in full gear. Next year I expect his poetry in my translation to be in print.

One thing I need to point out here is that it is not important to be a woman to translate a female poet, nor need one be a man to translate a male poet. It may help, for there are certain aspects of life that genders share. However, I have always liked the most to translate poems that speak of issues and moments in life that all human beings share and can understand. In addition, when I am translating a poet, I do not wish to know much about their personal life or the events that led to the creation of a piece. This approach gives me freedom or an open door to the piece itself, without any previous notions regarding what the piece is or may be about.

What can you say to those of us who have never visited Croatia about how the particular beauty of the land inspires its poets like Parun and Mihalić?

One really needs to visit and see it for themselves. Its strategic location is probably responsible for the history of the nation, and the natural wonders near and far from the seashore are extraordinary. No wonder people from around the world come to seek the sun, the sea, slower everyday life in the warm months of summer in the Mediterranean climate. Of particular interest is the fact that this relatively small country, the size of West Virginia, has a rather high number of poets, many of whom write about the inspiring beauty of their natural surroundings.

Has Parun's example inspired other Croatian women to make a career of it?

Vesna Parun is unique in that she was able to create masterpieces in sonnet form as well as in free verse. She wrote love lyrics, war poems, children's verse, dramas for radio and television, as well as satirical fables. In addition, she was a translator and an artist always remaining true to her calling and her independence. Such talent is rare. There are not very many women who could live only on writing in that part of the world and during the time period in which she lived. Much depends upon their family situation and support.

Some of the women whose poetry I translated in the past include: Vesna Krmpotić, Ljerka Car Matutinović, Adriana Škunca, Sonja Manojlović, Božica Jelušić, Anka Žagar, and Neda Miranda Blažević-Krietzman. Because of the country's size and location, many of its women poets are competent in more than one language and write translations for the Croatian journal *Most/Bridge*.

Any final thoughts about these poems by Vesna Parun and translating them?

These poems render life experiences of a human being as reflected in surrounding nature. For Vesna Parun, love is the most important thing that makes and keeps us human. Interactions with other human beings transform us and keep us changing, just as everything in nature around us changes. The sea best represents that continuous change and movement that life is. We are open to expectations and our anticipation brings forth fear and joy. Nature for Vesna Parun is not static outside the human sphere but parallel to it and dynamic, continually changing just like each human being. What we have in these poems is the vivid and memorable depiction of love/life experiences from a woman's perspective.

You With Hands More Innocent: Selected Poems of Vesna Parun
Translated by Dasha C. Nisula
Exile Editions, 2019

With this volume, readers in the English-speaking world have the chance to know what those in Croatia have known for three-quarters of a century: that Vesna Parun wrote the best love poems ever written in her language, and was—is, because her work lives—one of the most remarkable of 20th-century European poets. In truth she was much more than a poet, producing works in practically every genre of literature. But poetry is how she first made her name, and it is what she will probably be most remembered for. Parun is also important as an icon of female empowerment, being the first Croatian woman to live by and for her writing. At the time she set out to do this, in the war-torn 1940s, it was an incredibly brave and daring thing.

Her first book, *Dawns and Hurricanes* (1947), hit the postwar Croatian cultural scene like a burst of sunlight coming into a sick room. These are marvelously optimistic, sensual, vibrant, life-affirming verses, especially given when and where they came into being. From the beginning, her imagination is large, generous, empathetic. Take these lines from "I Was a Boy," where she recounts a night of dreams in which she assumes different forms:

I was a grape from a red cluster
in the teeth amidst kisses
a fox that ran out of a snare
a boy, who throws shouts with a sling;

The poem ends: "What haven't I been, what haven't I dared, / a mirror of a fish in the pupil of an otter?"

The love poems brought something new to Croatian literature, being from a woman's point of view. They are honest and poignant. In "Olives, Pomegranates and Clouds" she recounts an old story—waiting for a lover—making it fresh and vivid by letting a host of other sensations wash over her:

When I meet him on the road, I turn my face
after clouds
yet three days I waited by the fence for him
to pass.
Since, pomegranates have begun to bloom,
the sea has swelled.

As if to say, she too is blooming, her heart also is swelling. Farther on she says, "But already I am tortured by what is to come." The poem concludes: "Already three days behind the fence, full of youth, I wait / for your steps among the dark olive trees." Who is this idiot man who never shows up? Here is one enchanted reader who wishes he could take the man's place.

Born on the island of Zlarin off the Dalmatian coast of Croatia, Parun grew up surrounded by the sea, which figures prominently in her poetic imagery. One of the poems in this collection, "Before the Sea, As Before Death, I Have No Secret," is as good as its title, and there are a number of other standouts, such as "Harbour" and "A Coral Returned to the Sea."

While Parun pondered philosophical and spiritual questions throughout her career, they become more evident in her later poems, some of which also display more of a satirical wit. In the final poem in this volume, "Epilogue," from the book *Ashamed to Die* (1974), the combined feeling of reflection, melancholy and amusement reminds me somehow of the mixed autumnal moods of Shakespeare's later plays:

I shall never be
a trampled grass
and I will rustle clearly
so the children
understand me.
Who passes by me
will be happy.
And the bell, the old sinner,
will cease to toll.

I don't speak Croatian, so I am no judge of the fidelity of these translations by Dasha C. Nisula. However, I can judge their felicity and beauty in English. It takes a poet to translate a poet. Based on this volume by Parun and the volume of poetry she translated by another Croatian writer, Slavko Mihalić, we can surmise that Nisula is a fine poet in her own right, whether or not she ever produces any verses bearing her name. Thanks to her, Vesna Parun now lives in English as well as in Croatian. For this great gift we owe her our undying thanks. We should look forward with keen interest to whatever poetry she decides to translate next.

REVIEW | Jesi Buell

Haiti and the Homunculus

Charlotte and the Chickenman
Aina Hunter
Whisk(e)y Tit, 2022

Aina Hunter's haunted novel, *Charlotte and the Chickenman*, is a David Lynchian grotesque that unfolds in a surreality that hovers between dream and nightmare. Charlotte, the protagonist, oscillates between realities and identities throughout the book. Her fragmented nature is reflected in the world she inhabits that fractures into vignettes in different spaces and times. She moves between the

Haiti of the near-future (2048 to be precise) and moments in her past that span from her time at school to her inauspicious birth. The book reads like a fever dream fed by the anxiety of today: festering with horrible election results, an infectious virus, as well as maternal and/or ecological anxieties.

Race, sexuality, and gender are inextricably entwined in this book. Hunter is masterful in capturing the nuances of these identities, depicting them in across a full spectrum rather than the binary that most discourses center upon (i.e. black/white, gay/straight). Charlotte, whose name and age change throughout the story, is a light-skinned black woman who is bisexual and sometimes is described as masculine and others as feminine. The fact that she changes identities mirrors the fact that she lives in a nebulous world in-between the extremes of a binary. The intersectionality of Charlotte's identities truly capture what it is to not fit in squarely in any part of the constructed world. Shades of skin tone are seen fluctuating in the characters but also in the landscape. Parts of her world become 'white' spaces or 'black' spaces; 'female' or 'male'. The surreal nature of Hunter's prose allows the reader to explore these spaces as someone would who does not 'belong.'

Another common thread is pedophobia: a generalized anxiety, or sometimes even revulsion, towards children. At different moments, we see Charlotte struggle with her sexuality and being attracted to women in the same moments that she is aborting or losing a child. Several times, the fetus or embryo is referred to as a homunculus, an alchemical miniature but fully-formed human being. Like a golem, this is a constructed man used in folklore to illustrate an aberration of man's creation and to remind us about the dangers of 'playing God.' While not inherently evil, there is something nefarious about this creature and the connotation is important as Charlotte contemplates her baby or the idea of a baby. At one point, the characters discuss the fetus as a "hybrid tumor" or a "kind of sex tumor . . . [that] develops hair and fingernails as it grows . . . [and] [s]ometimes part of an eye or a tooth in random places." The thought of babies, unwanted babies, and gestation as a cancer is nothing new but, through the unorthodox narrative, Hunter gives us different angles of this thought. In this novel, we see the blood but we also see the magic.

Darkly humorous and kaleidoscopic, Hunter's prose is ultimately the reason to pick up this book. If you enjoy *Mulholland Drive* or Solondz's *Palindromes*, you will enjoy seeing their visual success made textual by this author with her adventurous and experimental form. It mirrors the odd times we live in and it can be dizzying and sad and scary, but ultimately Hunter manages to capture its beauty too.

REVIEW | REYoung

Whale of a Tale? Or Albatross?

Ahab (Sequels)
Pierre Senges
Translated by Jacob Siefring & Tegan Raleigh
Contra Mundum Press, 2022

Pierre Senges' *Ahab (Sequels)* is a belletrist's treasure trove, a language lover's dragon hoard. His prose is brilliant, beautiful and, at five hundred and fifty pages, bounteously so. The undrowned Captain Ahab pops to the surface like a "joyful champagne cork." We have "immense chandeliers, large as an octopus disappearing into the ceiling," "slices of smoked meat as numerous as the pages of a book." Word begets word, phrase begets phrase, metaphors cascade one upon another. "One metaphor and then two, then seventeen metaphors before the chapter's end . . . forests, clouds, stars, roses, hogs, tulips, flies, flour, a horse, some nacre (belonging to a pearl), Berenice's hair, Baubo's belly, some straw, a brook, another horse, (whinnying, that one), and a snaffle." This linguistic feast is conveyed by an equally rich sentence structure, Henry James on joy juice, clause compounding clause, parentheticals within parentheticals, barely restrained and oftentimes not by colons and semi-colons, one idea loosely connected to another by silken threads, free associations, digressions, catalogues, lists. "There is the walnut shell today, the gets started on the wrong foot today, the good tidings like the half of a mango today, the mosquito bite today, the mouthful of a brioche today, the smell of roasted chicken scented through the open window today, the headwind today, the letter in the box today, the silhouette without identity today, the violent sneezing today, the nap & meditation today, the strong alcohol today, the sudden rain today, the indeterminate remorse today, the almost pleasant melancholy today, the discovery today, the reconciliation with his childhood today, the reading a comforting page today . . ." And on it goes for a page and a half, and not necessarily comfortingly.

Senges likes lists, and he gives them to us, but not all lists are equal. Homeric and biblical lists convey provenance, genealogy, chronology, the vastness of armies, armadas. David Foster Wallace's Madame Psychosis (the brilliant metempsychosis of the ditzy but tragic Joelle) reading her lists of human deformities and abnormalities in a deadpan voice conveys the weight of her own psychic deadness. David Markson's absolute minimalist lists in *Reader's Block* force the reader to assign any and all values to the text and essentially write their own book. As Crocodile Dundee might say, *That's* a list. Senges is like a bastard child of Markson (*with* transitions), who says too little, and Henry James, too much. The narrative, or at least the prose, surges ahead, piling on more information before its premises and conjectures can be examined or challenged, and the question one begins to ask after fifty or one (or two or three or four) hundred pages of lists, catalogs and strings of metaphors is, to what end?

Comparisons have been made between Senges' *Ahab* and Huysman's *A Rebours*: *Against the Grain*, which has been described as a torrent of baroque descriptions and unending streams of rococo linguistic curlicues. It has also been said to lack any real dialogue, characters or plot. But even a glance at Huysman's Des Esseintes reveals a heartbeat, a living, breathing soul, and conveying that soul, a very human voice. No such life exists in Senges' Ahab. Melville's hero repeatedly proclaims himself a hollow man but he is also a force majeure seething with hatred and the desire for revenge. He curses the whale, blasphemes against God and, like Odysseus (and Sandokan), risks not only his own life but that of his ship and all his men. Senges' Old Ahab, on the other hand, truly is a hollow man. He never exhibits emotions, he is never angry or upset. All is calm, placid, the waters never roiled, no tempests. Even when negatively fraught words appear on the page they have no more value than washing instructions inside a shirt collar.

Unfortunately, this does little to engage the reader's interest. It also works against Senges' reconstruction of Melville's hero, whom he has divided into a post-whale Old Ahab and a pre-whale Young Ahab, and whom he elides respectively more than a century into the future (with dates in the margins to anchor us in time), for the purpose, it seems, of tracking Moby Dick's publishing history, from its poor reception, to its rediscovery, revival and ultimately its reincarnation as a screenplay for the movie version. But when we speak of Old Ahab and Young Ahab we are not talking about James Joyce bifurcated into the tormented young intellectual Stephen Dedalus and the older, world-weary but wiser Leopold Bloom. This is not the zygotic Jekyll and Hyde, curer of humanity's ills by day and monster by night. This is the simplest algebraic equation, $x=y$. Cow one *is* cow two. It may be true that we are always the same age inside, but we are still different at each stage of our lives. Senges' Old Ahab and Young Ahab are paper cutouts, distinguishable only by external attributes.

Setting forth on the sequels of the title, Old Ahab eschews the sea and anything related to it. "No way he's going to prepare fish filets or crack oysters and lay them out on a carpet of seaweed and ice." Instead he seeks lowly landlubber careers as he reinvents himself or is reinvented as a shoe shiner, kitchen hand, donut maker, elevator operator, priest and father confessor, in each case cloaked in comfortably familiar attributes of those occupations, "the tapestry of the elevator, the floor buttons, or the shiny spot on the elevator operator's shoe—and sometimes the collar of his uniform"; the cassock and distracted air of a parish priest hunkered down "between the wood walls of his confessional" as he listens to the tedious litany of greater and lesser sins. And in each case Ahab accepts his new role with the equanimity of a clothing store mannequin without bearing the least resentment toward or even awareness of the capitalist caste system that traps the everyman in these humble positions. One can argue, of course, that Senges' intent is not to expose social issues (and it isn't) but rather to demonstrate the process by which (cultural) information is transmitted through society and, in some cases, myths are made. In an inverse of the infinite monkey theorem, which results in the production of one book, Senges' one book produces an infinite number of somewhat better informed monkeys. Even far inland, the coal miner or hay farmer who knows nothing of the sea, who has never read or even heard of Captain Ahab, is imbued with knowledge of a man's (morbid) obsession with a great fish.

The pre-whale Young Ahab, on the other hand, is just setting out in the world. He meets the librettist DaPonte, experiments with metaphors, "he was hardly expecting to meet so many blasted metaphors" (nor were we), crosses the ocean to London, where he finds his way in theater, first as a stagehand and prompter and finally as an actor playing Shakespearean characters, all in preparation, one assumes, for his ultimate role as Captain Ahab, in the process allowing Senges to explore Melville's and his own fascination with the bard, including rumors of Shakespeare's involvement in the murder of Christopher Marlowe. But in taking the Young Ahab, as well as the reader, through the trapdoor from the substage onto the main stage, Senges also sets a trap for himself as he rehashes the worn postmodern trope of the murder of the characters by the author, of the author by the characters, Young Ahab murders Melville, Don Quixote murders Cervantes, the ghost of Sherlock Holmes murders Conan Doyle, Mary Shelley is murdered by the doctor (with the help of his creature), Philip Marlowe murders Raymond Chandler, etc. The bell has tolled for these deaths before.

The desire for vengeance and the "epic grudge" are at the heart of *Moby Dick* but in Senges' version the words revenge, grudge and the more innocuous (but no less insidious) *resentment* are mere ink on onionskin. We are initially told that Ahab bears no grudge toward the whale, that's all forgotten, in the past. It's the whale who can't let bygones be bygones, although the Mobester's desire for vengeance seems halfhearted and indiscriminate as he begins to dine on anyone and anything along the littoral that reminds him of his former tormentor Captain Ahab, whether in Cape Cod, China or Araby. A man strolling along the beach is "swallowed up by a whopper of an allegory." A charred pine log that only vaguely suggests Ahab's dark and austere figure meets a similar fate. It is only when Old Ahab attempts to capitalize on his story and he is buffeted about by the caprices of producers, writers, etc., that his long forgotten grudge against the whale is rekindled as a grudge against Hollywood and life as his original script is rewritten into an unrecognizable mishmash of Shakespearean and modern drama with the prospect of various famous actors auditioning for his role, some more plausible, others downright risible: Spencer Tracy, Charles Laughton, James Cagney, Buster Keaton(?!). Perhaps even more over-the-top, Cary Grant (*Moby, Moby, Moby . . .*). Slapstick aficionados may enjoy Senges' deserved send-off of Orson Welles who, asked to appear in the screen production, immediately assumes he will play Ahab (yes, absurd, he had already ballooned into a caricature of himself), until, that is, an ego-deflating meeting with the producers, lawyers, director, writers, et al, where they announce in gleeful unison that his role will be the whale! Adding insult to injury, he will be expected to wear an enormous whale costume. Ha, ha, funny, right? Unfortunately, we're not done yet as Senges moves on to—who's up next?—yep, Fred Astaire. One does, however, detect genuine resentment on the author's part when, pondering F. Scott Fitzgerald as a possible script writer for the story of the whale, the narrator impugns mostly modernist (and, one suspects, successful or at least popular) writers of what Senges calls "dry-bones fiction." "Now there's no doubt, that Fitzgerald's windows have gone dark, there weren't that many lights to turn off anyway." Hemingway is "born from the flank of a swordfish." Whatever their authors' personal failures, the "dry-bones fiction" of Fitzgerald's *Tender is the Night* and Hemingway's brilliant young trifecta sticks to this reader's ribs much tighter than Senges' bone-dry fiction.

And all the while the narrative goes back and forth in time, back and forth across the ocean, back and forth between characters and their occupations, frequently revisiting information the reader has been given before. One could argue this is intentionally tautological, recursive, that Senges is exploring parameters of literature received through the oral tradition. One could also generously call this wave action, mimicking the motion of waves for a lyrical effect. Too often, however, it simply feels repetitive. Throughout this unsteady voyage Senges presents us with cultural signposts, references to black-faced minstrelsy, jazz, newsboys, street traffic, but instead of a lush life it reads like a still life of Gershwin's NYC, the reportage of someone who has studied Americana but not lived it. There's no juke in the joint, no jizz in the jazz.

Which brings us back to the question, what does this all mean? Senges' Young Ahab "sees in metaphors a breach into other worlds, not the warp and woof of thought, but the interval between two ideas, the interval itself, the ideas mattering little, what does it matter if they even exist . . . " There is no rise and fall of temperament, the narrative does not plumb the depths of human emotion and experience, there is no *de profundis*, no Nautilus propulsion system driving us forward on a vital mission. Only words that evaporate as quickly as they are read, too often leaving the reader becalmed in the doldrums. All the seemingly wise sayings, the pithy, witty turns of phrase, the bon mots, the sardonic, the clever—as ephemeral as clouds in the sky, summer rain. Those who have had the dubious pleasure of listening to a schizophrenic or a speed freak will recognize the pattern. Initially everything seems to make sense and even sounds brilliant but it goes on and on until you realize there really is no connection between ideas except for tenuous transitions and the next cigarette.

Perhaps Senges felt it necessary to write a book equal in volume to Melville's to beat us into our senses (he's great!). The whale, alas, is less than the sum of its parts, a hot air balloon inflated by empty words. Ahab is an endless set of possibilities, both prequels and sequels, but never reifying into a satisfactory whole, which would be what—an aged, defeated, world-weary Ahab who has seen his life edited, rewritten and finally discarded by a bunch of Hollywood hacks? But Senges didn't write that. To be fair, if you enjoy cleverness for its own sake, if you like listening to a stand-up comic tossing out one-liners until the wee hours of the morning, you might enjoy Senges, all five hundred fifty pages. Fans of *Tristram Shandy* might even find shadows of Sterne in Senges' rarefied word play, although Uncle Toby on his hobby horse was a heckuva lot funnier.

In the end, who cares, right? Each to his cup or his kettle of fish or tea. The cause for concern lies in the fact that this sort of writing has claimed more space than it should (intellectual bullying? oh my!): writing that calls attention to itself without really knowing why; writing that stays on the surface, that does not care to dirty its hands or get its feet wet; what might also be called predatory or parasitic writing or even grave robbing, that exhumes the corpses of past writers, perhaps out of reverence but possibly just convenience because those who are guilty of these sins have nothing of their own to say, which is indeed a mystery. How can anyone who writes beautiful words as easily as a fish farts in water have nothing to say? Perhaps sensing an incompleteness himself, Senges seems to have difficulty in ending. There's a sense of his wanting to say more, the consummate *thing*, echoes, perhaps, of Beckett. However, when Senges says I can't go on, I'll go on, this reader's response is, stop, you're killing me.

A final note. It would be impossible to fairly and accurately assess Senges' work if it were not for the brilliant work of the translators, Jacob Siefring and Tegan Raleigh. Great translation is in itself an art, but also the product of due diligence scholarship and an unbounded curiosity about everything. Monsieur Senges and his readers have been well served.

WILL STANIER

MINOR CELEBRITIES

Cameramen of Her Majesty's Secret Service hold no allegiances,
an unfortunate fact with obvious, often terrible consequences.
Look no further than your local corner store and you'll see
what I mean: newspaper racks upended and the cashiers
all scampering about, nervously chewing on their fingernails.
I met one of Her Majesty's cameramen once in a shadowy
alleyway in Plymouth, South Dakota. Anyway, it was nothing
to write home about. While I'm at it, did you make sure
to feed my parrot? I left his grub pellets in a blue container
in the garage, behind the punching bag and next to the pool
equipment. I don't own a pool anymore, but I did when I
lived in France with the nephew of the President—the French
president, of course. Coco Chanel's step-daughter lived a few
doors down and sometimes we'd meet, just to shoot the breeze.

Maternal Instinct

My mother told me at an early age, "If you have children, I will take you out of my will."

I never had any children, but that wasn't the reason.

I never wanted to have children because (1) I didn't want to contribute to the planet's over-population (2) I didn't want to raise a child in a patriarchal, sexist and misogynist society and (3) you can't have intellectual discussions with them.

I am now 76 and have experienced the maternal instinct.

I have several deer who wander through my backyard munching on hedges, day lilies, hostas, arborvitae and anything else not sprayed with deer repellant on a daily basis.

This spring a mother left her newborn fawn by my porch.

I was quite concerned as the animal was out in the open with no protection.

I wondered why a mother would leave her baby. Was she a bad mother?

I called the Game Commission and several other agencies but got no reply, so I just hoped nature would take a good course.

I was especially worried if it were to stay there all night.

Night noises could be terrifying: screeches, yelps, snorts.

In the morning the fawn was gone.

No signs of a marauding intruder.

In the ensuing summer days, the fawn and several others grazed and munched with their mother.

They grew up fast, their star-like spots fading.

They became sure-footed and ate like their mother to my great consternation.

It is fall now and a young buck with velvety immature antlers visits almost daily.

When I watch it from my porch, it looks at me with vague curiosity. No flinching or tail flicking.

I am awaiting the next generation and revel in the fact I have but to enjoy my children from not so far.

Tyrone Williams

Diktat

O

pen, the leading edge of a front,

thou art
a bank of Cloud
above all clouds

Oz,
the leading edge of all Ozymandiases,

yea,
the leading edge of all yeahs, nebulous year of yearning . . .

and though the cuneiform crumbles into wedges of dust
and though the pencil rolls off an uneven table of contents
and though the tables of type are overthrown by the cyphers of cyberspace

thy prevail over thine enemies' carcasses dragged through lakes rivers oceans indelible ink

and all will be written down as the face of the leading edge of a front

disambiguates

one unique
one eunuch verse

Kat Meads

Encounter with a Text/Context

A Bodega/Bodega Bay visitor encounters no shortage of attractions. Rolling hills, picturesque harbors, sand, sea, starfish, barking seals and, for those of us who prefer our coastal towns misty, creep-in /creep-out fog. The schoolhouse-now-private-residence Hitchcock made famous can be peered at close range; the nearby church of St. Teresa of Avila, photographed by Ansel Adams a decade before its cameo in *The Birds*, can be entered at will and without faith. Available to both gawkers and consumers: hat shops, bait shops, surf shops, kite shops, platefuls of today's fresh catch served in restaurants wide and narrow, boats to rent, high/low hiking trails that thread through (pick your pleasure) spare or jagged terrain, and, this day, an estate sale in progress along Shoreline Highway—my first estate sale opportunity since the pandemic made communal browsing less joy than risk.

What is it about certain old books? The heft? The wide, wide margins? The no-stint-on-quality paper? The 1951 ninth reprint of Grace Margaret Morton's *The Arts of Costume and Personal Appearance* offered the above seductions, plus the allure of situational ironies: we, its potential buyers, were an unfashionable, near slovenly bunch, garbed to the person in an accessory Morton could not have foreseen: the face mask.

Author Morton, clothing authority and academic, taught at the University of Nebraska for more than twenty years, a home economics professor and chair of the textiles and clothing division. Her ascending, triple-threat career was cut short by sudden death in 1943, a scant few months after the original *Arts of Costume and Personal Appearance* was published. Prior to its publication, throughout the 1920s and thereafter, Morton's fashion advice and historical reports appeared in the *Journal of Home Economics* (e.g., "Psychology of Dress") and Extension newsletters (e.g., "Appreciating Grandmother's Handiwork"). She also lectured outside the classroom, in one instance speaking on the "Art in Dress" to the Omaha branch of the American Association of University Women in January 1924. Those articles and lectures, on campus and off, presumably amounted to short takes on material she expanded to fill the 400 pages of *The Arts of Costume and Personal Appearance*. The result is not a book that delays its intentions. On page one of her preface, Morton offers up the "eager hope" that the contents that follow will help raise the bar in women's fashion and establish a "higher standard of taste among people everywhere." She names among her target audience "students of home economics" who'd go on to teach the subject, "advisers in retail stores," and the more comprehensive category of "all those concerned with selecting, making, selling and wearing apparel." From the start, certain crusade fundamentals crosshatch the fabric of Morton's prose: the staunch belief that "taste" *can* be acquired; that women—despite restrictive "economies" and "irregularities" of face and figure—*can* improve their public presentation; that to achieve professional success and personal fulfillment, women *must* fit the mould ("The world still wants its women to conform to certain standards of beauty"). That said, no reward will come without considerable and continuous effort. And what of it? Morton is nothing if not a proselytizing disciple of the try hard/try harder school. To *fail* in effort not only dishonors the self, it inflicts injury on Beauty in its most abstract configuration, a dual disrespect Morton refuses to countenance.

Its inspirational ambitions notwithstanding, *The Arts of Costume and Personal Appearance* was issued as a textbook and fulfills the requirements of that niche. There are illustrations; there are summaries; there are glossaries; there are charts; there are Further Reading suggestions. Like every textbook worth its salt, there are subheads ("Expressiveness of Lines, Spaces and Shapes," "Chroma or Intensity," "The Silhouette," "Personal Attractiveness and Marriageability," "Sway-backs and Prominent Posteriors"). In addition to covering subjective topics the likes of "Understanding and Dressing to Temperament," Morton provides in depth, technical discussions of color and texture. To bolster her arguments, she cites painters (Botticelli, Ingres, Whistler, Titian, Cezanne, Gauguin, Van Gogh, Arthur Dow), of-the-era writers (Clare Booth, Fannie Hurst, Dorothy Thompson), costumed movie stars (Vivien Leigh as Lady Hamilton), fashion designers (Coco Chanel, "Madame Valentina," the "young," "intelligent," "resourceful" Edith Head), scientists, social psychologists, and in one instance First Lady Eleanor Roosevelt, praised for her "unflagging energy." The author provides daily and weekly plans for "cultivating self-made good looks" and a checklist of "equipment" necessary to pull off the job. "Wardrobe building" suggestions are supplied for a range of events/activities ("spectator sports," travel, "homemaking and chauffeuring," bridge parties, "formal teas") attended/undertaken by students, businesswomen, homemakers, empty nesters, the young, the "mature," the "thin" with "bony necks" and "prominent shoulder blades," the "near-stout" and the fully "stout," who must under no circumstance give in to the desire to wear "spike-heeled shoes," a blunder that will make their "feet look too slender to support a heavy body."

Published during wartime, *The Arts of Costume and Personal Appearance* acknowledges the "great economic crisis," "era of emergency," and ongoing "limitations and curtailments of materials to which civilians are accustomed." Morton shares the decision to omit colored illustrations "to keep the price of the book at a reasonable level," adding: "The author of a volume of this kind in which there are no color plates has a real problem in attempting to tell the things she wants to tell about color." A single show of petulance. Morton strongly believes that "personal appearance still plays a part in morale" and that "the enduring principles set down in this volume will carry over into the new world ahead." For those resistant to the morale argument, Morton has another up her sleeve:

> In these troubled times there are many who sorely need a sense of security and feeling of significance. May it not well be that the achieving of an idealized version of one's self through the best possible personal appearance may help to free the spirit and bring a sense of poise and adequacy without which no human can be really happy?

A fan of the royal we, on occasion Morton's language sweeps toward the flowery. In a discussion of rhythm as "the mainspring of fine costume":

> In its simplest form we can see rhythm in the ripple of waves . . . in the sequence of attitudes of a great dancer . . . In spiral arrangements, as of a seashell . . . We feel it in the horizontal movement of trimming on wide-skirted evening gowns; or in the undulating lines of a picture hat, as it dips in relation to the head and shoulders.

In a discussion of line:

> We enjoy horizontal line movement because it suggests the repose and quiet calm of the horizon, or sleeping animals, or flat, quiet, resting waters. We respond to vertical shapes . . . because they revive in us the feeling of stability and grandeur, of tall cliffs . . . We thrill to upward swirls and flowing drapery because it suggests vigorous plant growth or the fascination of rising flame.

There are also thrills to be gleaned from striking combinations of color: "Too much harmony, too much sweetness and ease pall upon us. We look for the unexpected, and in the mastery of some dissonant element we get a thrill of conquest."

Such flights of rapture, however, are rare. By and large Morton delivers crisp, direct description ("low, flabby busts") in straightforward diction ("Clothes should be chosen for the places we go . . . not for the places we would like to go"). With similar bluntness, she tells us: "Many women's hat problems are due to oversized heads . . . often caused by having too much hair, which should be thinned." The "average woman's taste in the choice of allover patterns is far from good"; "few women have the strength of personality . . . to wear large scale, bold prints"; and "although American women are conceded to have the best figures in the world" (who concedes this is unclear) "in many ways we fall far short of the standard." There is no ambiguity as to the "contemporary ideal" figure, defined by Morton as:

> Oval head and face; arms slender, sleek-muscled . . . shoulders and hips the same width, waistline well curved, thighs the same width as the hips . . . graceful, proportioned calves, slender ankles, and feet which, when standing, come together.

The "most enviable height"? Five feet five. Regarding the "flat-chested boyish figure of the 1920's with its debutante slouch and air of disillusionment"? Good riddance.

Confident in her mission, Morton's tone, which aims at encouragement, now and again descends to scold and reprimand: "All too few people today seem to have the particular brand of intelligence or skill to achieve results which may be said to embody style." "Those who claim that clothes bore them have surely failed to understand feminine psychology." And, for Morton, this obviously exasperating state of affairs: "Some young women of real ability fail to realize the value of a good appearance. Sometimes they are absorbed in intellectual pursuits and regard themselves superior to so-called feminine frivolities."

When criticizing a specific public someone, Morton characterizes rather than names: "a certain Swedish skater of stocky chest and arms"; "the short figure and bowed legs of one of Hollywood's beloved stars" (identified elsewhere as Bette Davis by less discreet Edith Head). Morton has no qualms about using "peasant" as pejorative and problem category ("Square, wide, peasant-like feet require shoes with broad, square toes and low heels") and does little to disguise her objection to "aggressive" females. For a color exercise, she tosses students a double-whammy challenge: come up with a "school dress" for a girl handicapped not only with the dread "aggressive nature" but also bodily "plump." Although accomplished women are lauded throughout the text, the author sticks to the premise that professional advancement can be achieved—and sustained—by the retiring and the demure. "Many a handsome face has been enhanced or marred by the mental attitude or the general philosophy behind it," she writes in the section that stresses the importance of maintaining a "pleasant facial expression." Approvingly she repeats *Vogue* editor Caroline Duer's distinction between wrinkles "of the skin" and "of the soul," the latter, in Morton's elaboration on theme, created by "holding grudges" or "being envious and uncharitable." For those unsure of how far they've fallen on the wrinkle index: "A study of one's face in good light without make-up may reveal selfish, pouting wrinkles or lines of anxiety or melancholy or fear." *If* "deep lines have developed between your eyes, try the use of 'frowners' at night. They can be had at any drugstore and have many times broken up this habit entirely." How to dispatch the afflictions of anxiety, melancholy, and fear Morton leaves to other texts and experts.

Morton's frowners advice appears as number eight in a list of nine "exercises" at the conclusion of chapter two. A great many of her exercises, chapters one through thirteen, make me extremely glad not to have occupied a seat in Morton's classroom or been at the mercy of her grading pen. A substantial number resemble *Buzzfeed*-style self-evaluation quizzes:

• Do you dress to win the approval of the opposite sex? Your own sex? As compensation? As self-expression? As escape?

• Analyze yourself to see if you can determine wherein you do or do not possess qualities of style.

• List your assets and liabilities to consider in working out your own personal problems (of proportion).

• Record . . . your voice . . . Is it harsh, strident, monotonous, or uncultivated?

Other assignments demand more time and talent:

• Plan and execute in water color or tempura paint a series of experiments demonstrating . . .

• Make a collection of costume accessories such as shoes, bags, gloves, belts, jewelry, etc., in which structure has significance and decoration is restrained, emphasizes structure and is well suited to its function.

• Explain the difference between stylish, stylized, taste, smartness, chic, being "in style," "having style," elegance, being elegantly dressed, dressy, cute . . . the spectacular, the banal, the dramatic. Illustrate those terms with examples.

The final example above bookends a chapter titled "The Meaning of Style," a probe into what style isn't ("making up one's face in public places") and is ("the choice of some tellingly effective ornament, not at once noticed, but, when noticed, not easily forgotten"). For the confused—or tremulous—another daunting "rule" to ponder: "Style is personality." Above all, the acquisition and maintenance of style requires "self-discipline," starting with the "self-discipline . . . to see that one is well scrubbed and brushed and polished and exercised, well-girdled, with carriage erect, no matter how persistent one's inclination to relaxation or indolence." To be very, very clear: there shalt be no slacking off—not today, not tomorrow, not *ever*.

Bombarded by dos and don'ts, I find I need a break and take it within view of where the very stylish Tippi Hedren/Melanie Daniels boated across Bodega Bay with her cage of lovebirds, attired in a pale green sheath dress with matching jacket, fur coat, silk scarf, suede gloves, heels, purse, and necklace of gold, courtesy of Morton favorite Edith Head. Reportedly, Head made six copies of the outfit to accommodate various stages of bird attack. The 1952 short story "The Birds," penned by Daphne du Maurier—no fashion slouch herself in those Cornwall sweater and slacks sets—features protagonist Nat Hocken, who had suffered a "wartime disability," works part-time on a nearby farm and can't comprehend why the persecuting birds have come to acquire the "instinct to destroy mankind with all the deft precision of machines." Hitchcock had reprinted Du Maurier's story in one of his *Alfred Hitchcock Presents* anthologies, but what reanimated his interest in the subject matter was a 1961 article published in the *Santa Cruz Sentinel* headlined: "Seabird Invasion Hits Coastal Homes," a report referenced in the film. For his 1963 production, Hitchcock kept Du Maurier's title, the coastal setting, the bird attacks, the pecked-to-death corpses, the escalating frenzy of attacker and prey, inept bureaucratic responses, house confinement, and of course the spookiness. Otherwise he glammed it up with socialite character Daniels, love interest/lawyer Mitch Brenner (Rod Taylor), open roads, and open waters. Du Maurier's tale starts claustrophobic and mostly stays that way, concluding with the working class Hocken family huddled in a dark, boarded-up house that may—or may not—withstand the next avian attack. In Hitchcock's film, the four primary characters make their getaway in Melanie's snazzy Aston-Martin.

No used book comes into one's hands without a shadow presence. The previous owner had paid three dollars and fifty cents more in 1951 (or thereafter) for the book I bought in 2021 for a dollar. During the course of her ownership, Helen Fiondella had married—if the clue of the added name Swindt in different ink can be trusted. Did Helen Fiondella Swindt agree with Grace Margaret Morton's assertion that "very few *normal* (my italics) young women do not look forward to marriage"? One wonders. With the lightest of pencil strokes, Helen checks the "Good Skin" section and underlines an entire paragraph on "good carriage" with instructions to "point . . . feet straight ahead . . . not at an angle" and thus prevent "waddling." She also underlines a lengthy paragraph on how to achieve a "sitting posture" that is "hygienic" and "also presents a good appearance and indicates good breeding" in which feet also figure, one foot to be placed "a little in advance of the other." Helen joins me again on page 48 for Morton's "Design Essentials" discussion and checks the sentence: "All of art is concerned with the organization of certain fundamental elements, called by moderns the 'plastic elements' . . . line, form and space, dark-light, color, and texture." Helen also endorses Morton's opinion that "no other element is so important to good costume" as line. Helen and her pencil return to number Morton's "stages in developing color appreciation" from "development of color sense" through "discernment and application of color principles" on page 131. On pages 137-38, Morton discusses the science of color, light, spectrums and artificial illumination, but Helen holds back her pencil until Morton offers the caveat: "Although these facts give us no direct help in the problem of combining colors, they do put value and meaning into whatever work we do with color." And then Helen and her pencil desert me for 150 pages, returning briefly, briefly to star Morton's conclusions on what constitutes "a masculine nature." Thereafter Helen

1) finds nothing more of note in Morton's textbook, 2) succumbs to the slouch of disillusionment, 3) stops reading by chance or by choice.

For whatever reason Helen exited Morton's text, I miss reading over her shoulder. I miss my mother too, who, in 1943, the year of Morton's first edition, was a four-year wife and first-time mother of an infant son, "Stretching the Clothing Dollar" by sewing not only the start-with-these-basics scarves and blouses Morton recommends, but dresses, coats, suits, and hats, an accomplished seamstress since her teens. Were she still alive, I could call and get her take on Morton's take of "reefer-type" coats and "fluttering chiffon." I could remind her of the college summer an admiring French woman waylaid me on a Paris street to ask whether I'd sell, for a handsome price, my "one-of-a-kind" denim skirt fashioned from a bell-bottomed pair of sailor jeans. I could remind her a chic Parisian had recognized the craft and ingenuity of her design and execution—ingenuity that, war-tested and wary, my mother continued to keep in play, even when times turned less hard than once they'd been.

Thomas Walton

Unsavory Thoughts

Leon Uris Is My Favorite Author

The last time I was in jail it was November. The streets were wet and from the cell that I was in you could see the rain beading on the windows of the cars parked down below.

It wasn't a cell really. It was a big room, a holding tank: the drunk tank. It was a fish tank for drunks, and it's true it was difficult to breathe. The rain and grey light through the narrow, metal-reinforced windows added to the claustrophobia in the tank, the sense of drowning. All the fish wore orange. It was a goldfish tank.

To be clear, I wasn't a drunk. Sure, I had *been* drunk directly preceding my arrest, but I wasn't *a* drunk. It would be an insult to drunks if I identified as one. Something like cultural appropriation. I was only twenty-seven, a novice, I rarely drank in the morning (unless I'd been drinking all night and it just happened to be morning).

It was the only jail I've ever been in that had windows the prisoners could look out. I suppose that sounds humane, to have windows to look out, but after I noticed I could see the café on 2nd and Jackson, the one I used to go to when I worked downtown, after I noticed that, I stopped looking out the window at the world that was now shut-off from me.

I had been in jail enough times to know that you could ask for books. When the food trays came, I asked a guard, very quietly, if he could get me one. In jail, people who read are considered, well, gay. I don't usually mind when people think I'm gay, (it does happen, I'm from southern Indiana, where they also think you're gay if you read), but jail isn't exactly the best place to be thought of that way.

The Bible might be the only book you can read in jail and not be thought of as gay.

"A book?" the guard said, suspiciously.

"Yes, please."

"What kind of book?"

"Anything is fine."

"Like the Bible?"

"Sure, if that's all you have, but really anything's fine."

The guard seemed to think about it for a while, and then said, "I'll see what I can do."

I never saw him again.

A few hours later a different guard opened the door.

"Walton!"

Walton means essentially, "foreigner," and in jail I never felt so aptly named. I was a foreigner there. Jail and southern Indiana aren't the only places I feel like a foreigner, but they are two of the least desirable. I'm guessing a few others also felt like foreigners there, but I wouldn't know. I tried not to talk to anyone if I could help it. Jail isn't exactly, for me anyway, my preferred place to make friends. Talking to people in jail is generally considered . . . well, you get the picture.

"Walton!"

As I walked over to the door, I thought maybe I was being released. Perhaps someone had bailed me out. But who? I didn't call anyone to tell them I was in jail. I was trying to think who might have found out I was there. I purposely didn't tell my girlfriend, for fear she might dump me, which she did anyway. Maybe she found out somehow, and overcame her shock and disappointment to forgive me and bail me out. I was thinking how wonderful she was, what a fine gesture it was, when I got to the door.

"You wanted a book?" the guard said.

"Ahh," I said, disappointed not to be released, "yes, please."

"Will this do?" he slid a book through the slot in the steel door. I didn't recognize the title, or author, but it was a book and I couldn't care less what kind of book it was. The fact that it wasn't the Bible was a relief. I just needed to read, to escape. I wasn't looking for moral instruction or origin stories. I was well aware of how I wound up there. In jail. The book he handed me was some sort of mystery or thriller. I could tell by the overtly symbolic objects arranged on the cover—a seal or stamp of some kind, white gloves—and the font dripping blood.

"Yes, perfect, thanks."

I walked back over to my bunk, of which my bed took up the lower half. On the upper half lived an enormous man who barely fit into his orange outfit. He was lying on his side, looking at me. I lowered my eyes and looked at the book. When I got to my bunk, I crawled under his fat belly that hung like a curtain over the side. Every time the food trays came, this man grunted and huffed and coughed a phlegmy cough as he climbed down from above. His huge, fat stomach flapping down the rungs of the ladder. I tried not to make eye contact with him, or his stomach, or any part of anyone else for that matter.

I read that book cover to cover. And then started reading it again. I was chain-reading, hotboxing it. I never left my bed the rest of the time I was there. Three days it turned out. I stopped eating. I refused my food tray. My bunkmate noticed and asked if he could eat it. "Yes." He traded my whole tray one night for a cigarette butt someone had somehow smuggled in. I tried not to wonder how they'd done it, and how it must've tasted when my bunkmate smoked it.

Sometimes now I think about buying that book, or checking it out from the library. I sort of miss it. Like you might miss macaroni and cheese, or chicken soup. It was one of the most important books I've ever held in my hands.

Empty, Void, Hole or Pit?

It makes little sense why life should be so painful. Until you consider gravity's constant, unrelenting pressure. It is the supreme oppression. I think this is why it's so easy for us to feel as if we're victims. Because we are. All of us. How could we not be in such a world?

I do wonder if certain political upheavals are at their foundations more about a vague sense of oppression, a gravitational oppression or general discontent. We're primed for insurrection. There's always time to add the specific issues of revolt later. How easy it is to rally others with slogans asking for change when all of us are trapped by the laws of physics. I'm surprised there aren't more Christianias, more CHOPs, more Nimbins, more Jan Sixes and more October Revolutions. To where got the Grateful Dead parking lot? I suppose we have fentanyl now.

In this I think I'm aligned with Pascal, who knew well the forces of gravity. I can't relate to those who do not walk around with that huge black boot weighing on their necks. Space is not the right word. Nor infinity. Not empty, void, hole or pit. All our shuffled lexicon's unable to describe it.

Perhaps I'm being too linguistic. For some people language is only a tool with which to buy beans or bread at the market. But for those of us concerned with affecting the sense of beauty—that is, for those of us concerned with art—language is a midden of empty shells left after our attempts to cast spells that would trick a moment into lasting forever.

I suppose you could also just go swimming. After all, what need is there for revolution, or writing, when the water's fine and the breeze is right? I'm guessing no one ever stormed a castle who knew how to surf.

These Are the Things I Can Do Without

They put a bank where the gay bar was. I'd say that pretty much sums it up. What's happened to the neighborhood. To the city, really. It was a dive bar. Everybody went there.

It was a fantastic place. By which I mean to say it was a dump. A dark and filthy hole. Fantastic. They had food but you wouldn't want to eat it. You didn't go there for the food. You went there for the cheap drinks or the sex, or both. We went there for the drinks, and the jukebox.

They still had an old-school jukebox, and you could play just about any song you could think of, as long as it was gay. Five songs for a dollar, which when you're drunk enough, seems like a great deal. They had Madonna, Cher, Barbara Streisand, Rick Izaaks, George Michael, Culture Club, "YMCA", etc. All the classic hits. We mostly played Queen or Morrisey.

One night with Jordan—who was going through a breakup—we played all the Chet Baker songs they had. I think it cost us ten bucks, a double album. There were some drunk queens in drag who were pissed, "oh honey this man is so depressing," they yelled at the beginning of each song. "Play some Diana Ross will you, puh leeze!" but we'd already made our selections and they complained for an hour and more about how you can't dance to "this jazz shit or whatever it is. Honey what *is* this!"

After "My Funny Valentine" one of them yelled at the bartender, "Sweetie bring me another drink before I slit my wrists." The whole bar laughed, and Jordan was cured of his broken heart.

But that's all done. There's a bank there now and nobody plays music or gives hand jobs in the booth near the bathroom while Tears for Fears sings "Shout. Shout. Let it all out . . . "

When the bank opened, they put a pride flag in the window for a few months, as a sort of gesture of respect I guess, but they eventually took it down. Sometimes when I walk by there I can still hear the music, "You shouldn't have to sell your soul."

Lee Upton

Nude Modeling for Introverts
by Medusa

Listen, I'm five thousand years old and have snakes for hair and am I shy?

Wear a hat. That's what I do. You can wear a mask too.

Now that you're vaccinated it's time to go out and bare at least some of yourself—to be more, you know, body positive and art loving. And while you're modeling it's a good idea to think about other things—like about people who want to cut your head off and put your head in a bag and how you're not going to let them.

If seeing you turns men into stone that's their problem. Some people would be lucky to be turned into stone, some people don't realize how lucky it is to be turned into stone . . . People look better as stone, last longer, decorate the plaza.

Remember, you're modeling truth.

It's not true that I am currently living in a bag and am pulled out when some guy's enemies approach. People make up stories because of that one time at a party when I kept putting my leg over people's shoulders. As if everybody hasn't done that. Besides, it was my party!

Again, wear a hat. If your hat squirms tell people you've got a lot of thoughts and your thoughts are busy, busy, busy!

Just think: you're ready to get out into the world and you have nothing to hide and no one to envy. You no longer have to watch endless Netflix comedies about people drinking in bars . . .

Again, that rumor about my demise is all wrong. Especially the part about how a horse jumped out of me while I was bleeding. How do I know? Decades after you've given birth to a child the haunting continues. In back of the cupboard: cereal bowl with two cheerios ossified into cement. In attic: ancient baby monitor suddenly speaks in strange voices. An abandoned breast pump chop-runs across your utility shelf. One tiny baby sock turns up inside your bra! If my offspring was a horse there would still be evidence!

Remember: Your cat isn't nervous about being nude, so why should you be fussy? Admit that during the pandemic your cat has established new parameters for your behavior: feeding on the half hour, treats ordered online, including weird toys with tassels . . . Admit that during the pandemic you became like a bartender for your cat. Except not paid, never tipped, always on call. Realize that you're doing this nude modeling for yourself, not only to pay for your cat's excessive demands.

Just a warning: Don't even peek at whatever those art students are drawing while staring at your body for far too long! Believe me, no one will capture your essence. Frankly, I myself would like to be represented in more flattering ways. Possibly, once in a while, I'd like to be represented with my mouth closed.

Again, you're serving art and artists! As for me, it's not like I'm looking for trouble. People come to me. Aggressive people. With swords. I let my head do the work that my hands won't.

A little secret about the golden fleece. It's fleas—that's what's glittering.

Julian Stannard

Three Poems

Summer Pudding

My mother gave me a summer pudding
to take to my sister
who lives on the other side of the heath.

Take it to the other side of the heath
without letting the juices spill
or the pudding drop.
Keep your arms out like so.

If Veronica tries to get it
tell her I'll shoot her from morning to noon
and then I'll shoot her from noon to midnight.

The gun's in the shed, oiled up and pumping.
Here, off you go, I have a bottle of gin
that's waiting to be drunk.
I have my fly swat at the ready.

I walk across the heath which is full of ferns.
Green is the colour of the heath in summer
when the rain has fallen and the sun has shone.

There are swathes of purple
and Hollyhocks and Lad's Love and Rue
and Sorrel and there's a couple of lesbians
with Great Danes.

A stag leaps out from behind a tree
and hundreds and hundreds of rabbit ears are twitching.
I'm about halfway now, holding out the pudding
in its purple glory on a lovely plate.

In the olden days
kings were crowned with summer puddings.

Ethelred the Unready are you ready?
    Not quite.

I know Veronica's out there somewhere
lurking behind the ferns.
Full of scratches and itches.
The ground strewn with bottles
and the steaming shit of a horse
swarming with strange bug life.

I found her asleep once:
an old mole chewing her foot.
a copy of *Dead Souls*
tucked under her head—almost happy.

I'm in sight of my sister's house
and Veronica's heathy breath
makes my ears tingle and my arms ache.
Ah the summer pudding she says.
I knew it was time.
All the summing fruits jostling at a debutante's party.
She's drooling like a dog.
Your debutante days are over, I say.

I've been waiting for it behind the ferns.
No Veronica, fuck off, you can't have any.
Oh but I will, I will and she's tugging at my trousers
and my sister's on the stoop shouting
Keep going! Keep going!
Veronica, please, I'm almost there.
She says, I'm having that fecund pudding.

THUD

The blind boy had a lover
who was ravenous. A raven?
How would he know?
Her mouth hungry as a puppy
her arms so plucky, lucky.

He couldn't see whether
he was on the Inner Circle or the Outer.

He couldn't see the People's Palace.
He couldn't see Buchanan Street.
He couldn't see the Clyde.

He could hear the wind. He could hear the gulls.
He could hear the thud of a ball.
He could hear the chanting—
his lover tied herself to his foot
her hair was black of course.

NOX PERPETUA

He wanted to make a film. He enrolled on a course.
Federico Fellini, Rosselini, Bolognini, Pasolini
and Stevie Wonder rolled into one,

the *mise-en-abyme*, the universal scream.
He was interrogating the existential hole
not some cameo role—

He hatched a plan and flipped a fugue—
Break into the Kelvingrove Gallery
under the cover of night, perpetual night
and steal Dali's *Crucifixion*.

No thorns, no blood, no nails
suspended above a lake—
ready to slide into the lake.

First they went to Mother India to eat—
to work out the ins and outs.
Kenny slapped a paratha
round his face, an instant balaclava.

Powder your face with sunshine
Put on a great big smile . . .

They lowered Christ of Saint John of the Cross
onto the boy's back.
He had broad shoulders,
his calf muscles strengthened
by amorous trysts.

Tricky getting out of the door.

And he walked down Argyle Street
as if it were Palm Sunday
with sixty million pounds of Salvador Dali
    on his back—

Tricky getting back into the flat
with Christ of Saint John of the Cross on his back—
The neighbours gawping.

But there's always a chance
with Christ on your back
of a MIRACOLO fast track.
The boy got his sight back!

Raven lay on her back, aflutter. Ecstatic boy.
He was the lead man in his own film.
He'd acquired the gift of sight.
He'd thumbed his nose at the police.
He'd gotten away with a Crucifixion.
There was trouble, however, with his erection.

He clambered onto the raven
like a winged aardvark
heavy, locked in, soft—

No nails in his hands
Christ slid down the cross
into the lovers' bed.
A *ménage a trois*. A thud.

A kitsch triptych.

Imagine there's no heaven.
Quite easy if you try.

A short film—
it won several prizes.

The *Osservatore Romano*
said it was shot through
with a slither of evil.

Miss Lady Macbeth

Son of Charles flew to Belfast, hired a car
and drove to a farm where they sold him
a tiny dog. Tiny dog now back in London.
Shepherd's Bush if you please—

The dog was too tiny to leap onto the sofa
which somehow thwarts the reason for being a dog.
So Charles built a ramp, a tiny dog-to-sofa ramp.

And that might have been the end of it
were it not for the fact that tiny is now the word
of the day, the word of the month and catching.

The two cats, small, are smaller now.
Lady Macbeth becoming Miss Lady Macbeth.
The mice laughed at her, tiny laughs if you will.

The books in Charles' house have begun to shrink:
pocketbooks, some the size of postage stamps.
The Brothers Karamazov a walnut whip.
Pop it in your mouth, won't have to read it now.

And the cigarettes so very tiny too.
You're smoking three packets a day
just to keep your hand in.

Or lie there on the sofa saying Fuck it!
watching tiny dog climbing the ramp
and wondering if the wife's not shrinking too,
to fit in, tiny, why not?

Oh titchy tiny dog, let's call him Toni, Toni Macaroni
tiny barks, tiny licks of the ear, tiny everything

M.J. Nicholls

Dinas Dinlle to Edern

Roughly and arbitrarily excerpted from the forthcoming novel *Condemned to Cymru: An Abecedarian Achronological Picaresque* (Sagging Meniscus, May 2022)

Dinas Dinlle

A hollow sensation. The sea.

Dolgarrog

Sometimes I worry when I am forking spaghetti into my maw that I think precisely nothing for weeks on end.

Dolmelinllyn

"Sometimes when we're screwing I imagine inserting a screwdriver up your anus," Katrin said.

Dolwyddelan

I receive a card every Valentine's Day from my mother, with a picture of a heart inside a 'no entry' sign and the caption below: "Remember, no one will ever love you." No matter where I am in the world, this card always seems to reach me, like a light-hearted parental cudgelling in the face. She claims that the card is intended to keep me facing cold hard reality, and rescue me from the futile and time-sucking pain of pining for women who will never fuck me. She might have a point and I hate her.

Downing

I would like to purchase a coffee that shows in the foam the haggard and defeated expression I wear at having capitulated to the chokehold of cut-throat capitalism without the merest yelp of protest.

Drefach

Helga, here are five things I would do to secure a flecklet of your ardour:

1. Talk up the virtues of Right Said Fred to a Crip.

2. Divebomb naked into a croc-dense swamp.

3. Rate each crisp in order of saltiness, flavour, adherence to their advertised shape, and bulkiness in the bag.

4. Listen to Dylan's *Down in the Groove* on a loop for seven hours.

5. Crawl into a damp crevice.

Drope

Have I been?

Drury

There is no point in pretending. Gallic post-rock outfit Call Me Loretta should have been bigger.

Dryslwyn

I met Katrin the eighth time in a Greek restaurant. Over a bowl of moussaka, she told me that her father was flatulent and aloof.

Dulas

Sorry, Miki Berenyi, I had to burst you.

DWYGYFYLCHI

'Fear' from Barrie Bartmel's *Poems of a Poltroon* (p.30):

> fear of change
> fear of change
> fear of change
> fear of change
> fear of change
> fear of change
> fear of change
> fear of change
> fear of change
> fear of change
> fear of change
> fear of change
> fear of change

DYLIFE

It was late. I had necked seven whiskies and a limeade chaser. In a haze of burp, I recalled in italics the horror of being born . . . *your first human contact the rubbered hands of a yawning locum who without permission snips your half of the umbilical cord; the wan overhead lighting in the room bringing no real sense of theatre to the occasion; the realisation after five seconds that you have been forced into existence with no prior consultation and that your mother is a selfish and uncaring asshole you instantly loathe; the notable lack of oohs and aahs in the room indicating you are either hideously formed or that very few people care you are now here; your mother's failure to overcome her own exasperation to fake a pleased smile now that you are swaddled in her sweaty arms; your fondness for the layer of amniotic fluid and blood that will never henceforth sheen upon on your skin; the sheer torture of no longer being safely encased in a heavenly womb where your room and board is provided free of charge; worrying that you might have to present your National Insurance Number to the locum when you haven't the capacity to read letters or numbers yet; not being told about Tom Waits so assuming everyone everywhere and everything everyplace is completely pointless;*

the smug look of an unidentified relative that says 'I can play hopscotch like a boss, and you are a mewling bundle of goo'; your mother's face clearly worrying that you will turn into a pathetic failure and lifelong financial burden and that she should have signed up to that zoology course instead; the six minutes that have elapsed in which the father has failed to present himself; the concern that crying loudly is your natural state, and that you might be crying loudly for the rest of your life; that surge of suicidal panic when your arms desperately reach for the snipped umbilical cord so you can swiftly hang yourself . . .

DYSERTH

Sometimes the afternoon trickles with uncompromising exactitude into a bog.

EARLSWOOD

"I sex up media in the East Wales area. I use manipulative images to entice users into clicking on content. If you wanted to be unkind, you might call me a clickbait artist. For example, say I want to yoke a reader into looking at how they might save £500 on their insurance premium. I deploy a picture of a young lady with large breasts. Or, if I want to show how an old man managed to escape a gang of robbers, I deploy a picture of a young lady with large breasts. This is my profession. I am a leader in my field," Timothy Hall said to me.

EAST WILLIAMSTON

There is a plaque here outside the shop where Bob Holness once bought a colander.

EDERN

My mother mistook the waspish cynicism of a bourgeois feminist for a solid foundation of unconditional love and support. It happens.

Dum-Dum Theory

We were trying to figure out how we got here. Not location—I'm here; Zeke's there; Eli's elsewhere. You are, too. Everybody is. We were trying to figure out how we ended up where we are, apart, without any agreement on what *here* is.

We all agreed about the technology—the bodies and spaces and the health and safety protocols, some of them at least—but we were advanced, Zeke, Eli and me. We were following the signals to the source, the last time everyone was on the same page in the same place.

The motorcade came around the bend slow. We weren't there. We were still in the substance when it happened, but through the miracle of modern machinery we were able to watch it all together apart, over and over again. Zeke paused the film where he always did.

"This was the last point at which we could all agree," he said.

We agreed. The car turned, passed behind a sign whose signs were on the other side, and when it reemerged, the bossman had an arm in front of his face. The bossman's lady was leaning toward him. Something was clearly wrong. Zeke paused again.

"And this is where the disagreement begins," he said.

"For example," said Eli, "she was not hot."

We were well familiar with Eli's opinions on the bossman's lady, but the miracle of modern machinery meant we couldn't stop him. He was the meeting's host, the one with the reliable connection, the reason we kept him around if you could call it around.

"It's," he said, "it's gaslighting. They treat it as a given she was beautiful and glamorous, the epitome of class, but she was ugly. Eyes so far apart they were on the side of her head, amphibious. Even her own bossman didn't want anything to do with her. Nothing like our bossman's wife, who they say is not hot, but who is."

He didn't mean the ladybird; he meant the wife of the current bossman, the real one, ours. We don't recognize their bossman same as they didn't recognize ours. Anyway you can see her tiddies if you tweak your machine just right.

"We don't disagree with you on that," Zeke said.

"Well somebody does," said Eli. "Everybody else but us."

"Nonetheless," said Zeke, "she already looked the way she looked before the last point at which we could all agree."

"Tadpole," said Eli. "Toad dressed in a strawberry sheetcake. Not an inch of skin in sight."

"My point," said Zeke, "is that she looked essentially the same before as after. Different colors and fabrics. Minor variations in the bob. But the same eyes, same visage, same overall shape on the twenty-second as the twenty-third. This is a private disagreement, individual, not world-historical. Although, again, we agree with you."

Before Eli could reply, Zeke had the film going again. I, for one, was unprepared, but it was always something of a surprise when the bossman's brain flapped back from his skull, and then forward, a slab of gray baloney. He kept it running as the bossman's lady climbed over the back seat, the guard strained toward the trunk, before it looped back to the beginning. Zeke stopped it before the sign. There was no more firsthand information than there ever was. We were forced to rely on "experts."

The experts had many theories, but really they had two. The first one we grouped under the umbrella term "complexity theory." There were many variations, but complexity theory posited that some combination of racketeers, palace guards, paramilitary, and freelance communists had collaborated to collapse the bossman's head and alter the course of history, the fabric of reality. Zeke's emphases changed from day-to-day, balances tipping depending on his mood or some information he had gleaned on the darkside of his machine, but he was always and squarely in the complex camp. He liked his webs tangled, his mysteries wrapped up in enigmas, wheels within wheels.

Alternatively, we had "simplicity theory," the lone rifleman with the magic bullets. Simplicity theory was not as simple as it seemed—the rifleman would have had to lock, load, and unload at near-inhuman speed, the bullets to perform impossible feats of perforation and repenetration. Zeke had not coined the name to denote the sequence of actions the theory posited; no, he thought that anyone who embraced it was simple-minded. He never said this directly to Eli, who was all in on simplicity theory, but it was clear enough in his manner. For his part, Eli seemed to gravitate toward simplicity because theory itself detracted from what he considered the real concern, which was naked pictures of the real, our, bossman's lady.

Even now he was sharing one on the screen. I hadn't seen it before. Neither Zeke or I had any idea how he kept coming up with them. In this one, she waved an AR-15 one-armed while a stream of what looked to be piss fell from between her legs, individual drops bouncing up from the white-tiled floor, frozen in high definition, spattering her bare feet. The piss so focal that it was a minute before I noticed the swastika pasties

over her nipples. Zeke quickly replaced it with the original video.

"Destroy that image," he said. "Wipe your machine memory. It could be used as evidence to support the feverish fantasies of our enemies."

Of course, the enemy did not technically need the imagery to support their fantasies, and the idea that we were not being surveilled made Zeke sound like an adherent of simplicity theory. Everyone lived on faith alone, a steady diet of symbolic gesture—the enemy, Eli, even Zeke. Everyone but me. I was meant to break the tie.

For years I had been meant to break the tie, but neither complexity nor simplicity appealed to me. Complexity theory treated the world as simple, and simplicity theory made it too complex. At one point I figured I'd never get around to deciding—journey as destination and whatnot. It gave us something to do, and no one seemed to mind.

But recently a few of our guys had caused some trouble, stormed the palace in silly costumes and had themselves a little parade. No harm no foul was how I saw it. In fact, some of those pictures kind of cracked me up. But the other team said it had cracked the foundations of the Republic and defiled the sanctity of our secular temple or somesuch. Both, of course, could not be true. We had a new urgency in getting answers; we had to figure out how the old bossman died and quick. It was our job to reassert a consensus on reality, and as tiebreaker it would ultimately fall to me. Fortunately, Eli's picture had given me an idea.

"Get that filth back on the screen," I said.

"Et tu, Tom-Tom?" said Zeke.

"Bear with me," I said. "Eli?"

At first I thought that Eli had misunderstood me. Filth. Bare with me. Because the next thing we saw on screen was Eli's dick. But it had all happened too quickly. He was already naked and erect. It looked huge, but I think that was a trick of perspective. He probably still had the images up on his own machine and had been cranking that hog the whole time.

"Goddammit," said Zeke, "what is this colloquy coming to!"

"The other filth, Eli," I said. "The bossman's lady."

The purple head bobbed toward and away as he tried to find the share button, but all was soon well, and I resolved to pass over the preceding few moments in silence. The still was back on the screen.

"Can you magnify it, Eli?" I said.

Eli zoomed in, toward the crotch, naturally. But the crotch couldn't tell us anything. It might have been any crotch.

"Not the crotch," I said. "The pee. The pee on the ground, where it's splashing back up."

"So that's your thing?" said Zeke.

"Good enough for the bossman," said Eli.

"Bossman doesn't have a piss fetish," I said. "Everybody knows he's a germophobe."

"Urine is sterile," said Eli. "Ever find yourself with a gaping wound and no disinfectant you just get somebody to pee on you."

"Sounds like you're the one with the fetish," I said.

"I got *aaaall* the kinks," said Eli.

"Long as it doesn't involve actual human contact," said Zeke.

For a second it felt just like old times, like we could have kept up the riffing forever. But old times were gone. There were documents to be analyzed, decisions to be made, epiphanies to wallow in, though I didn't know that yet, just had a hunch.

"This isn't about sex," I said. "It's about the pee. Look, those drops cast a shadow."

I gave them a minute to take it in, then told Eli to zoom up to the tits, the nipples in particular. Just as I'd expected—the electrical tape they'd used to make the swastikas had texture and gleam.

"These aren't the sexy parts," said Eli, but I deduced from the delay when I told him to move up to the face that he had maintained his arousal and was probably on the verge of climax.

There it was. The dark, squinty eyes. The almost-archaic smile that failed to indicate any particular emotion. The mass of wavy hair. What there was not was any indication that the head had been surgically implanted, that the photo had been doctored.

"You're the expert, Eli. What do you say?" I said.

Eli was still panting as his mic came back on. He answered between gasps.

"I never did know her to be into nazi stuff," he said, "and boobs can vary in size at different parts of a woman's cycle, not to mention time of life. Wax job is meticulous like you'd expect with her. Abs look great. It all checks out for me."

"Just what are you getting at, Tom-Tom?" said Zeke.

"We all know," I said, "that our bossman's, the real bossman's, lady did not pose for that photograph, and yet Zeke and I agree that it's real. It's real; it just never happened."

"And what does that have to do with the purpose of this meeting?" said Zeke.

"Put the film back on," I said. "Slow it down so we can watch it frame-by-frame."

He did so, and as the car crawled forward, I told them what was on my mind.

"The motorcade never actually moved this slowly, and yet here we are, watching it, because that's what we want to see. What we won't see is a bullet. The Carcano has a muzzle velocity of 700 meters-per-second, down to 550 at 100 yards. Zapruder's camera recorded the shooting at 18.3 frames-per-second. It's no surprise that the bullet isn't captured on film, but it isn't impossible that it could have been. What I'm proposing is that Eli's photo exists, not because it ever happened, but because the other side wants to believe our bossman is into fascism and watersports, and because certain guys on our side, Eli, for example, actually are into fascism and watersports."

The old bossman's brain was flapping very slowly now, defying laws of motion.

"In the same way, this footage exists because it needed to. Maybe a gun fired, maybe several, maybe none at all. Maybe a bullet hit him; maybe it didn't. The bossman's brain exploded because somebody needed his brain to explode. Anyway, that's my vote."

There was silence from the other nodes. Zeke neglected to pause the film and it cycled through again, another thing that never happened but that we witnessed every day. The limousine inched toward the sign. In that time, I allowed myself to imagine I'd convinced them, that together we would convince the world. I wasn't sure Eli would be able to get his brain around anything that didn't include his dick, but I knew Zeke was capable, if he could get over the fact that I hadn't voted his way.

It turned out he couldn't.

"That," he said, "is retarded, Tom-Tom. I'm going to call it dum-dum theory, after you. I'm gonna call you Dum-Dum."

I stood my ground.

"Just a few months back, a bunch of our guys had a party in the palace and the other team said they beat one of the guards to death with a fire extinguisher. Video all over the place, no sign of a fire extinguisher, no real sign of violence at all. Coroner's report said no blunt trauma. That guard died because somebody had to die. You gotta let go of complexity, Zeke. Cause and effect got nothing to do with it. Happening has nothing to do with it. They turned reality itself into a machine."

As soon as I said it, I lost the connection. At first I worried Zeke or Eli had cut me off, but we'd had rowdier discussions over the years, and Zeke had just vowed to call me Dum-Dum, implying a continuation of our relations. I tried to rejoin and got no signal. I suspected Zeke and Eli were blocked too. I had come too close to power. Whoever had been listening to us knew I had cracked the code.

But it was too late for power. Power's done. As soon as I put what they were doing into words, the system crumbled, cause and effect came rushing back in. For example, I wanted to reconnect with my friends, but I could not make that happen just by wishing for it. I could not make it happen at all. Maybe my friends were never real. Maybe they had only existed because I wanted them to.

This is true for you, too. Try standing outside and wishing for death with all your heart like I did when I realized I would never be able to connect with Zeke and Eli again. Doesn't work anymore, does it? From now on we have to get our naked pictures the old-fashion way. Meet up. Point and shoot. The meet up, that's the hard part. We will all only ever live or die by blunt trauma and stray projectile at the end of a vast conspiracy or random act of rage. No more wishing makes it so. And this is all thanks to me.

Goddammit I miss my friends.

Andrea: an existential parable on first love

I.

My first love shows up to my door; this gorgeous German
girl named Andrea from several decades ago asking me if
I can somehow help to locate myself showing me a photo
probing me if I can recognize who i was (a romantic
teenager) not knowing i used to be this handsome
glowing, passionate, self-loathing Jew, brooding
& blue, curious, inquisitive in a fisherman's sweater
(a transitional object I never took off which reminded
me of her & that phase of first love) her not knowing
my heritage (for some strange reason feeling a profound
amount of guilt & shame) keeping it secret being innocently
self-conscious, all too aware of previous historical carnage
& conflict, not wanting to chance it nor wanting to lose her
starting to fall in love with her, making it all that much more
intriguing & intrinsically complicated, intense & overwhelming

II.

Just home from college during the holidays spending
hours contemplating & wandering through the snowy
suburbs, isolated, melancholy in the strange silent solitude
of the seasons whose placidity (in an ethereal, fictional way)
seemed to separate one phase of my reality from the other
from those once selfsame forms & images of everyday
functioning to the sudden spontaneity of a surreal love
& fantasy & if time stood still so did these intense feelings
of beauty; nothing could possibly feel more lovely or lonely
that fragile feeling of falling madly for this gorgeous stranger
(now an obscure fugitive on-the-run from all those obvious
oppressive things of culture meant to mold & manipulate me)
spending days vacillating between her presence & trepidation
of the eternal, timeless universe; core essence of quintessential

quietude of our time on earth, strolling over soft stone bridges
above rising swollen rivers of Winter, roaming past crackling
frozen, babbling brooks winding through the whispering woods
whose distant echoes & murmurs sifting through the snowy
pachysandra took on a sense of redemption & forgiveness
(even revelation) developing its own language of transcendent
stimulation (whose brooding & rumination turned to
a pleasant sublimation) dissecting the intimate, tender
details of nature, amplifying & opening the senses

III.

Other peoples' fireplaces welcoming & taking me in
the rin-tin-tin drip-drip-drip purple rivulets of water
having melted & now streaming on that one warm
holy day feeling like I could hear the whole universe
meditating, praying, opening & closing like some
sacred stamen of a flower, flowing down the gutters
from the shutters of the village; the minutes, the hours
of the clock tower & cathedrals & funeral homes
& barrooms & alleys; the tumbling flakes of snow
suddenly showing up out of nowhere falling like
a miracle from the heavens making snow angels
at midnight with this stranger I felt like I knew
forever, brooding & blissful in the moment
in love; in love with all that ethereal snow
coming down with a town finally shut down
& not a living soul around the sound of no sound
at all & silent nights gradually flowing into silent
mornings, slowly, gradually gathering & building
up on the delicate eyelashes of all those sad, old, poor, pouting
horses, lined up in a row with heads lowered from head to tail
still graceful, modest, mournful, tearful across from
right in front of the park, feeling like the only one in the world
who made eye contact & really gave a damn looking beat down
depressed, down on their luck, of which I always felt without even
being aware of it akin, so sympathetic, dreaming of shooting all
those abusive, soulless lawn jockeys, aloof & arrogant, right
through their tourist top hats, while letting them all go
on one final insane trot & mad dash for freedom

IV.

The chattering teeth of the wild wicked wind whipping against
my iridescent, glowing, crystal lattice, having spent a whole
absurd existence, whether real or imagined, seeking elusive
illusory sanctuary with opaque, pastel pink & blue skylines
materializing from my mind through the shattered branches
of mythological, collapsible, the tender
twinkle of twilight slightly creeping through bleak, beautiful,
solitary, sighing windowpanes welcoming stray winds from
the wild, mystical, mysterious outside mixed with mollifying
blasts of heat from the beat & rhythm of the radiator whose
cacophonous symphony seemed to say everything would be
alright wrapping me up & warming up my insides; the slight
creaking of trees laden with snow bending in the breeze like
antique country dining room tables whose fissures got narrower
& wider due to the subtle change of weather; all those different
 varieties & variations & metaphysical forms of sacred silences

V.

With girls like this anything seemed possible, like some blissful fable
able to instantly shake off all those pathetic, petty problems in life
which might plague, even frighten us & the natural phenomenon
of hearing ourselves for the first time breathe aloud, something we
had been holding in for so damn long & maybe all it really came
down to in the long-run was the sentimental nostalgia & splendid
ritual of it just being our song or our brand of beer in cozy pubs
helping to quell all anxiety & stress & fear looking back at it
as some queer, romantic
brilliant bittersweet
bad buzz when your song comes up later on over the radio
realizing life is just about that sole magical moment, a mood
you're in, somewhere between lust & love caring nothing
at all about making the distinction & ditching & escaping
& taking off with that sudden fleeting feeling of freedom
& liberation from a damaged history of overbearing, psychological
& spiritual subjugation as far as it would take me & never returning

VI.

When she many years later showed me a photo of myself
as this thoughtful, sensitive, introspective young adult, asking
if I recognized this individual I just very mechanically replied
quite literally & philosophically that I did
secret soulful part of my sentimental, palpitating spirit start
to creep up from deep within & flare up once again & when she
took off started to go into something of an emotional, uncontrollable,
trembling, hysterical
originally left me in the first place for reasons & circumstances
beyond my control due to a domineering father & deferential
mother (with guilt & conflict) making it very difficult & virtually
impossible to break from due to these selfsame feelings of 'a guilty
conflicted soul' that i was not 'deserving of it' & constantly internalizing
that 'I was wrong' or what Freud alluded to in those cogent psychodynamics
of profound triangulation if one has not taken the proper, necessary steps
towards self-reflection or individuation not simply only dating your partner
but having to take on as well the burden & responsibility of multiple members
leaving one to experience that overwhelming phenomenon & sensation &
 exact feeling & emotion of what it means to be keenly & 'strangely deserted'
 acutely alienated & abandoned; in fact the microcosm &
 the complexities of what true love is (her pure sweet existence the keen
sublimation of the result of all those very challenging & difficult things
in what it meant to cope) while the simple motion of putting my head
down on the pillow never felt quite so natural & pure, having entered
the 'sweet dreams' of existence, shrugging off all that pain & suffering
& becoming the real-life personification of that proverb of what it feels
in essence to be the perverse dynamic of 'forgotten & forgiven' (devoid
of 'identity & being') & all of those ridiculous things preceding this . . .

David Collard

The End of All Fiction

Forbidden Line
Paul Stanbridge
Galley Beggar, 2017

The Encyclopaedia of St Arbuc
st-arbuc.co.uk

In March 2019 I received an unusually brief email from the novelist Alex Pheby which contained nothing more than a link, with neither content nor comment. Clicking on it took me to the homepage of something called the *Encyclopaedia of St Arbuc*. I had no idea what it was, although it looked, somehow, *official*.

It was, I learned from Alex, the work of the author Paul Stanbridge, whose first novel *Forbidden Line* so impressed Neil Griffiths, founder of the Republic of Consciousness Prize, that he added a last-minute 'First Novel' category to the inaugural shortlist, solely to accommodate Stanbridge (who unsurprisingly won in that category). Here's what Neil said at the time:

> A modern day *Don Quixote* channeling early Wittgenstein and late Heidegger, and the events of the Peasant's Revolt, *Forbidden Line* take us on a picaresque journey through Essex and London in what must be the most exuberant and maximalist novel of ideas ever written in English. It really shouldn't work, but it does so with a kind joy and comic panache that few writers possess. It's an achievement to be admired, relished, and loved. [. . .] This isn't magical realism—it's so much more mysterious and profound than that.

Picaresque, exuberant and maximalist it certainly is. I'd add that it's breathtakingly funny.

What *Forbidden Line* may first bring to mind is 'Pierre Menard, Author of the Quixote', the great short story by Borges originally published in 1939, a tale that anticipates and subverts the tendencies of literary post-modernism. In fact Menard's imaginary grandchildren crop up briefly towards the end of *Forbidden Line* in an episode featuring one Ian McEwan, who is clearly *the* Ian McEwan.

In Stanbridge's take, the maniac autodidact Donald J Waswill (Don) and his doltish companion Isaiah Olm (abbreviated as 'Is' throughout) leave their home in a redundant Colchester water tower to embark on a shambolic, low-budget odyssey during which they run into drunks, crusties, dignitaries, the Essex constabulary and feuding locals until, somehow, managing to fetch up in London. On their travels a hefty home-made case containing Don's Encyclopedic life work is repeatedly destroyed, only to reappear intact, its contents miraculously unharmed.

Stanbridge's Don is every bit as deranged and single-minded as his Spanish prototype—obsessed with a metaphysical phenomenon he calls 'the hyperfine transition of hydrogen' and in thrall to Lady Chance, a capricious secular deity who dictates his every move. He and Is undergo a series of encounters with the contemporary world—our world—which are beautifully rendered and as funny as anything in Flaubert's *Bouvard et Pecuchet* or Beckett's *Mercier and Camier*, two other farcical masterpieces, both featuring incompatible male compadres. Is cannot read or write (unless the plot requires him to do so, when he can do so with ease) but has the same gift of total mental recall as Funes the Memorious (another Borges link, from the *Ficciones*), and so functions as Don's recording angel, a lumpen Boswell.

What impresses is Stanbridge's elegant, eccentric and richly rewarding prose coupled with his unflagging invention. The lyrical descriptions of backwater Essex are consistently lovely, and there's a sophisticated philosophical undertow with Wittgenstein, Heidegger and Lucien Lévy-Bruhl in attendance. There are lots of very good jokes, elaborate digressions, pointless repetitions, countless literary references, passages in Greek and Anglo-Saxon and Middle English, sudden violent reversals, dazzling rhetorical flights and, throughout, a sense of unalloyed authorial joy in the whole project.

While he is unafraid to court tedium (thoughtfully inviting the reader to skip such passages when they crop up), Stanbridge has the rare gift—vanishingly rare—of making his reader (this reader, at any rate) laugh out loud, and regularly. Chapter 27 reduced me to a chuckling puddle when, at one point, Don and Is discuss what they respectively pronounce as 'déjà vu' and 'deja-vu', leading to a wonderful *mis en abyme* in which simultaneous hypothetical déjà vus (or deja-vus) are giddily embedded, one within another, leading inevitably to 'an eternal stasis of the hyperfine transition of hydrogen' until a baffled Is throws in the towel:

—What you are saying is so far over my head, said Is, that it has ice on it.

Forbidden Line is both very, very silly and as wholly and profoundly serious as Cervantes' original. It's hugely entertaining and deeply satisfying and unforcedly weird—a rich plum pudding of a novel, but a plum pudding with antlers.

When I first met the author I was disappointed to hear that he'd abandoned plans for a second novel, which was to have been entitled *St Arbucs*. This was bad news to me as an admirer but, as it later turned out, Stanbridge was at the time fully committed to writing something, but not a novel. Something else entirely.

Which brings us back to the *Encyclopaedia of St Arbuc*.

How can I begin to write about this extraordinary text? It has to be read online and is not available in print, and if it were it would be a book the size of the world. You have to see it for yourself (at st-arbuc.co.uk) to get an idea of the scale and scope and implications of this astonishing project.

If you haven't already clicked (and are therefore down the rabbit hole and unlikely to return for some time) you should know that it's described on the landing page as 'an immaterial text', something defined as 'an item of linguistic discourse which has no physical manifestation as writing or sound'.

It takes the form of an alternative Wikipedia, a mass of online documents dedicated largely to affairs in the failed city state of St Arbuc. I don't want to say much more than that because I'd hate to pre-empt the thrill of personal discovery when you log on for yourself.

Thanks to multiple internal links, and further links to the internet beyond itself, and thanks to the option of reading random consecutive pages (which I recommend), no two readers will ever have the same experience of the text. Like *Finnegans Wake* (which is a thoroughly material text in its most familiar incarnation), the *Encyclopaedia of St Arbuc* is a work of jaw-dropping originality and of seemingly inexhaustible complexity. The permutations are practically limitless.

There are several recurring characters: Bally Parts, Jaylad Politis, Rebert E. Benhole, David-Cream and, strikingly, the Prince of St. Arbuc, whose name is half a million words long and given in full, in caps, in a single Encyclopaedia entry that's longer than *War and Peace*. There are fantastically elaborate digressions worthy of Sterne, and further digressions within those digressions, and an enormous index page with links to entries which can be navigated alphabetically or (again, recommended) at random. There is even a plot of sorts, although that emerges slowly. What impresses above all, apart from the content, is the design and delivery of what began as a conventional novel and has become a benchmark in contemporary experimental writing.

The electively anonymous author himself has no control over, or stake in, the fate of his text, which can be edited (like Wikipedia) by *anyone*. (A couple of recent additions to the Index page are product placements for a range of hair products, and why not?)

It's immersive, compelling, frustrating, dazzlingly original and deeply unsettling. I've been exploring the site haphazardly for the past two years and feel I have barely scratched the surface. While other writers have staked a claim in this territory, notably Borges in his short fiction 'Tlön, Uqbar, Orbis Tertius' (1940), the *Encyclopaedia of St Arbuc* is, in its conception, and execution, an imaginary world on an epic, comprehensive and finely detailed scale.

It appeared without fanfare. There was no launch, no publicity, no reviews anywhere—none of the usual publishing practices. Indeed, apart from a website acknowledgement to the Arts Council for funding, no publisher seems to have been involved and, as a new take on the production and distribution of fiction, it appears to mark the beginning of the end of conventional publishing. The article you are now reading is among the tiny handful of pieces prompted by Stanbridge's text, and if you go online and do a Google search for 'St Arbuc' you'll be taken straight to the coffee shop franchise and will have to dig deep to find any reference to the near eponymous (but entirely unrelated) St Arbuc.

Like *Forbidden Line*, its more conventional predecessor, the *Encyclopaedia* is richly and profoundly comic but also, despite its literary self-awareness, far harder hard to pin down than its predecessor. Like *Finnegans Wake* it is certain to attract fanatical devotees and dismay the unadventurous. Perhaps, and also like *Finnegans Wake*, it will amount to no more than a wonderful cul-de-sac.

When I last heard from the author he said he had completed a true second novel, 'a satirical, barbarous version of *In Memoriam*, narrated by two rivers and a horse'. The title? *My Mind To Me A Kingdom Is*, which comes from a poem first published in 1588 and usually attributed to Edward Dyer. Here's the first verse:

> My mind to me a kingdom is;
> Such present joys therein I find,
> That it excels all other bliss
> That earth affords or grows by kind:
> Though much I want that most would have,
> Yet still my mind forbids to crave.

The mind as a source of consolation and happiness. Now there's a theme.

Contributors

Paolo Albani is the author of collections of short stories and curious encyclopedic repertoires on imaginary languages, anomalous sciences, unobtainable books, anomalous institutes, crackpots and involuntary comedians. He is a member of OPLEPO (the Italian homologous to the French OULIPO) and Magnificent Consul of Pataphysics, and is the editor of *Nuova Techne*, a magazine of literary and non-literary oddities. He collaborates with the Italian nation-wide magazine *Domenica de il Sole 24 ore*.

Greg Bem is a poet and librarian in Seattle.

Jesi Buell is an artist from Upstate New York. Under the name Jesi Bender, she helms KERNPUNKT Press, a home for experimental writing. She is the author of *KINDERKRANKENHAUS* (SM, 2021) and *The Book of the Last Word* (Whiskey Tit ,2019).

Marvin Cohen is the author of many novels, plays, and collections of essays, stories, and poems. He lives on the Lower East Side of Manhattan.

David Collard is a writer, critic and researcher. A regular contributor to the *Times Literary Supplement*, the *Literary Review* and many other publications, he organizes and hosts cultish online gatherings. His book on Joyce's cultural legacy, *Multiple Joyce*, is due from Sagging Meniscus on Bloomsday 2022.

Marc Estrin's world line approximates a cross between a fungal mycelium and a Rube Goldberg device. Biologist, theater director, EMT, Unitarian minister, physician assistant, puppeteer, political activist, college professor, cellist and conductor, he is baffling, even unto himself.

Jack Foley's numerous books of poetry, fiction and criticism include *Visions and Affiliations*, a "chronoencyclopedia" of California poetry from 1940 to 2005, *Grief Songs* (Sagging Meniscus, 2017) and *When Sleep Comes* (SM, 2020). He lives in Oakland and hosts a weekly radio show, *Cover to Cover*, on Berkeley's Pacifica station, KPFA.

David Henningham is an author, bookbinder and publisher. He is co-founder with Ping Henningham of Henningham Family Press.

Kurt Luchs is the author of *Falling in the Direction of Up* (SM, 2020), *One of These Things Is Not Like the Other* (Finishing Line Press, 2019), and the humor collection *It's Funny Until Someone Loses an Eye (Then It's Really Funny)* (SM, 2017). He lives in Michigan.

Carl Landauer taught history at Yale, Stanford, and McGill. He has written broadly on intellectual and cultural history and the history of law. He has published articles and book reviews in *Salmagundi*, *Renaissance Quarterly*, *Yale Journal of Law & the Humanities*, *German Studies Review*, *Confrontations*, *Beat Scene*, *American Scholar*, the *San Francisco Chronicle*, *Newsday*, and *Poetry Flash*.

Kit Maude is a translator based in Buenos Aires. He has translated dozens of Latin American writers for a wide array of publications and writes reviews for *Ñ*, *Otra Parte* and the *Times Literary Supplement*.

Kat Meads's essays have appeared in *Full Stop*, *New England Review*, *AGNI online* and elsewhere. Her most recent book publication, *Dear DeeDee*, is an epistolary memoir addressed to a nonexistent niece.

Kathleen Nicholls is an author and illustrator, best known for *Go Your Crohn Way*, the first of three books loosely based on her own experiences with chronic illness. She lives and works in central Scotland.

M.J. Nicholls is the author of the novels *Trimming England* (SM, 2021), *Scotland Before the Bomb* (SM, 2019), *The 1002nd Book to Read Before You Die* (SM, 2018), *The Quiddity of Delusion* (SM, 2017), *The House of Writers* (SM, 2016), and *A Postmodern Belch* (2014). He lives in Glasgow.

Bobby Parrott was obviously placed on this planet in error. In his own words, "The intentions of trees are a form of loneliness we climb like a ladder." His poems appear or are forthcoming in *Spoon River Poetry Review*, *RHINO Poetry*, *Atticus Review*, *The Hopper*, *Poetic Sun*, *Clade Song*, *Rabid Oak*, and elsewhere. He currently finds himself immersed in a forest-spun jacket of toy dirigibles, dreaming himself out of formlessness in the chartreuse meditation capsule called Fort Collins, Colorado where he lives with his houseplant Zebrina and his wind-up robot Nordstrom.

Paolo Pergola is the author of *Passaggi—avventure di un autostoppista (Rides: The Adventures of a Hitchhiker)* (Exorma, 2013), *Attraverso la finestra di Snell (Through Snell's Window)* (Italo Svevo Edizione, 2019), and *Reset* (SM, 2021). His work has appeared in several Italian literary

gazines. He is a member of OPLEPO/Opificio di
eratura Potenziale (Workshop of Potential Litera-
e), Italy's equivalent of France's OULIPO. He lives in
scany and works as a zoologist.

eph D. Reich is a social worker who lives with his
e and son in Vermont. He is the author of numer-
s poetry collections.

Young is the author of Unbabbling (1997), Margarito
l the Snowman (2016), Inflation (2019), The Ironsmith: A
e of Obsession, Compulsion and Delusion (2020) and Zol
20). He continues to reside in a limestone cave
ep below the city of Austin, Texas.

nela Ryder is the author of two novels-in-stories,
rection of Drift and Paradise Field, and the short story
lection, A Tendency to Be Gone. Her work has been
blished in many literary journals including The
arterly, Bellevue Literary Review, Prairie Schooner, Unsaid,
ska Quarterly Review, Black Warrior Review, Gulf Coast,
ant, and Conjunctions.

riana Sández (Buenos Aires, 1973) is a writer and
tural administrator. She studied Literature in
enos Aires, English Literature in Manchester, and
npleted a Masters in Literary Theory and Compar-
ve Literature in Barcelona. She runs the Literature
partment for the Friends Association of the Na-
nal Museum of Fine Art having previously held the
ne role for the Museum of Latin American Art of
enos Aires and other institutions. She writes for the
as supplement of La Nación newspaper and Revista Ñ
he Clarín newspaper. She has published a collec-
n of interviews and essays, El cine de Manuel: Un recor-
o sobre la obra de Manuel Antín [Manuel's cinema: an over-
w of the work of Manuel Antín] (2010) and the story col-
tion Algunas familias normales [Some normal families]
16). She has won awards for her stories in Ar-
ntina and Spain. In 2016 she received a grant from
National Fund for the Arts in the Creation category
inish Una casa llena de gente.

borah Bachels Schmidt lives in El Sobrante, CA
h her husband, Daniel and dog (read spiritual
de), Hazel. She has published a chapbook, The Milky
ath of Stars, and has a chapbook, Stumbling into Grace,
thcoming from Orchard Street Press. She has also
tten a memoir about growing up in Taos, Land of My
hantment; a children's book; and two genealogical
ventures, The Bible, the Ship and the Pewter Plate and The
norah in the Closet.

Will Stanier currently lives in Tucson where he is
training to be a librarian. He is the author of a chapbook, Everything Happens Next (Blue Arrangements,
2021). His poems have appeared, or are forthcoming,
in Cleaver Magazine, Interim, Pacifica, Lazy Susan, The
Volta, and RECLINER.

Julian Stannard is the author of Rina's War (Peterloo
Poets, 2001), The Red Zone (Peterloo Poets, 2007), The
Parrots of Villa Gruber Discover Lapis Lazuli (Salmon Poetry,
2011), The Street of Perfect Love (Worple Press, 2014), What
were you thinking? (CB Editions, 2016), Sottoripa: Genoese
Poems (Canneto Editore, 2018), Average Is the New Fantas-
tico (Green Bottle Press, 2019), and Heat Wave (Salt,
2020). Stannard's study of Basil Bunting was published by the Liverpool University Press (2014). He is a
Reader in English and Creative Writing at the University of Winchester (UK).

Aug Stone writes words and music, sometimes together. He writes for The Quietus & The Comics Journal
and performs absurdist comedy as Young Southpaw.

Christian TeBordo has published four novels and two
collections of short fiction. A new novel, The Apology, is
forthcoming this fall from Astrophil Press at the University of South Dakota. He lives and teaches in
Chicago.

Lee Upton's poetry has appeared in The New Yorker, The
New Republic, Poetry, and in many other journals as well
as three editions of Best American Poetry. She is the author of books of poetry, fiction, and literary criticism.
Her seventh book of poetry, The Day Every Day Is, won
the 2021 Saturnalia Prize and is forthcoming from Saturnalia in 2023.

Thomas Walton is the author of four books: Good
Morning Bonecrusher! (Spuyten Duyvil, 2021), All the Use-
less Things Are Mine (SM, 2020), The World Is All That Does
Befall Us (Ravenna Press, 2019), and, with Elizabeth
Cooperman, The Last Mosaic (SM, 2018). He lives in
Seattle.

Tyrone Williams teaches literature and literary theory at Xavier University in Cincinnati Ohio. He is the
author of several books and chapbooks.

Connie Woodring, a 76-year-old retired therapist,
has had many poems published in over 30 journals,
including one nominated for the 2017 Pushcart Prize.

www.ingramcontent.com/pod-product-compliance
Lightning Source LLC
Chambersburg PA
CBHW080252280626
47159CB00020B/3454